WinterMaejic

Also by Terie Garrison

AutumnQuest

Forthcoming by Terie Garrison

SpringFire

SummerDanse

WinterMaejic

Terie Garrison

Woodbury, Minnesota

First Edition
First Printing, 2007

Book design by Steffani Chambers
Cover design by Gavin Dayton Duffy
Cover image © 2006 PictureQuest
Editing by Rhiannon Ross

Flux, an imprint of Llewellyn Publications

The Cataloging-in-Publication Data for *WinterMaejic* is on file at the Library of Congress.
 ISBN-13: 978-0-7387-1028-0
 ISBN-10: 0-7387-1028-8

Flux
Llewellyn Publications
A Division of Llewellyn Worldwide, Ltd.
2143 Wooddale Drive, Dept. 0-7387-1028-8
Woodbury, MN 55125-2989, U.S.A.
www.fluxnow.com

Printed in the United States of America

To

Mrs. Erelene Christensen, Hilltop High School
Dr. Sharon Yaap Caballero, Hilltop High School
and
Dr. Alida Allison, San Diego State University

*"It is the supreme art of the teacher
to awaken joy in creative expression and knowledge."*
—Albert Einstein—

Acknowledgements

Thanks, as ever, to the members of the
South Manchester Writers' Workshop,
who make magic happen every week.

And to Sally. Always.

The Candles

Week 1	Peace	Ivory	Ginger
Week 2	Honesty	Pink	Sweet Pea
Week 3	Resourcefulness	Blue	Rosemary
Week 4	Strength	Forest Green	Sage
Week 5	Clarity	Lavender	Thyme
Week 6	Health	Pale Green	Melon
Week 7	Diligence	White	Carnation
Week 8	Creativity	Orange	Orange
Week 9	Generosity	Purple	Lavender
Week 10	Kindness	Yellow	Lemon
Week 11	Humility	Turquoise	Berry
Week 12	Love	Red	Cinnamon

The Candlesticks

Autumn	Water	Silver
Winter	Earth	Copper
Spring	Air	Crystal
Summer	Fire	Gold

-from The Book of Lore

✦

Maejic is a difficult gift with which to be blessed. Or cursed. I should know, for I have lived with it for eighty years and more. I wonder now whether being the leader of a vital mage community is sufficient recompense for my sacrifices. Would it not have been easier to deny this . . . this . . . this skill and immerse myself in the safer realm of magic?

But it is too late—far too late—to change my course. I have a new task ahead of me now, one entirely unexpected and not altogether savory. For a powerful new mage has appeared, and it has fallen to me to train her.

Her raw talent leaves me speechless and, all unknowing, she has done things few mages have the power to do. I know I should consider it an honor to teach her. But I begin to doubt that I have it within me. When she first appeared, I suppose I was harsh with her. But in truth, you can scarcely blame me. For, full sixty years too late, I found myself face to face with my soul mate.

Oпe

✦

"Hey, that's brilliant!" ten-year-old Traz said to me, his big brown eyes shining. "Do it again!"

I cocked my eyebrows at him mischievously, then looked back at the fire. It took only a moment for the anger I still felt toward Yallick to course through me again, and as I stared, the flames turned green. And stayed that way this time.

An idea occurred to me, and with scarcely another thought, I held my hands cupped in front of me. I imagined some of the flames flowing into them, and they did. A moment later I held a glowing green ball of light.

Traz's jaw dropped, and his eyes widened. I couldn't help smiling: Traz was hard to impress.

The ball didn't burn at all, although it made my palms tingle. I held it in front of my face and looked through it. Traz still stared at me, and through the green light, his face looked sickly.

Without warning, I tossed the ball at him. Quick as lightning, he raised his staff, and when the light hit it, the ball burst into thousands of bright sparks.

Before either of us could say a word, the door of the cottage opened and Yallick strode in. The grumpy old mage barely glanced at us as he closed the door behind him, took off his cloak, and hung it on the row of pegs.

"I have told you before," Yallick said in his gravelly voice, "that I do not wish for you to play with fire."

Beside me, Traz let out a small noise as he tried to hold in a snicker. I had to bite the inside of my cheek to keep from laughing myself.

"You," Yallick said, his gaze falling onto Traz, "go outside and gather up kindling. And then bring in some more firewood. You shall be staying here for supper tonight. And you, Donavah," I looked straight into his icy, blue-green eyes without flinching, "please go to your room and continue translating the manuscript I sent you last night."

I gave him a small nod, but waited until Traz passed me on his way out before I actually moved. I had agreed to let Yallick become my teacher, and I was learning a lot, but I still felt uncomfortable around his unpredictable moods. Whenever possible, I tried to exert some small degree of my own will in a vain effort to feel more like a partner than a student.

In my room, I sat at my desk under the wide window that looked out across the back garden. My eyes flicked back and forth between the manuscript of herbal lore, the lexicon, and my translation. Absorbed in the pleasure of unlocking the treasure of knowledge for myself, I completely lost track of time.

A sudden sound of click-clacking outside startled me. If it was already time for Traz's training session, it must also be time for my afternoon meditation. I still didn't understand why Traz didn't have to meditate. At Roylinn, everyone from Master Foris down to the youngest serving girls and boys had to take morning and mid-afternoon meditation. But once when I'd asked Yallick why Traz didn't have to, he'd said that it was none of my business and directed my attention back to the star chart I'd been studying.

I looked out my window to find Traz and Klemma, the martial arts instructor, just outside. They were working with staffs today, and as usual, Traz used the one he'd found when we were traveling together. Not that we'd known it had any special powers at the time; we'd thought it was just a really good walking stick. Now, each time Traz's staff crashed against Klemma's as he blocked a move or tried to get past her defenses, I winced. But the staff always came through the most aggressive of sessions without even a scratch.

As I watched, Klemma stepped backwards, and Traz danced toward her. He swung his staff low, then up under Klemma's outstretched arms. The tip of the weapon touched Klemma's breastbone, and with a yip of delight, Traz sprang back and raised it into the air.

"I gotcha!" he cried.

Klemma smiled at the boy, small for his ten years. "Indeed you did. Of course, your opponent won't always be obvious about leaving you an opening," Traz's face fell, "but you're catching on very quickly." His smile reappeared. "Very quickly, indeed. Now, again."

They both assumed battle stances. I enjoyed watching Traz train, and I looked forward to beginning my own martial arts lessons, but for now, I needed to find someplace quiet to meditate. I reached into my desk drawer, grabbed two taper candles without paying any attention at all to which ones they were, and went into the front room. No sign of Yallick, so I went outside. And immediately returned to get my heavy cloak. Winter was almost here and despite the bright sunshine, it was cold outside.

I followed a path into the wood that led in the opposite direction from where Traz and Klemma were making all their racket. About a fifteen-minute walk from the cottage, there was a meditation shelter that I loved to use when weather permitted. The shelter had been carved from the bottom half of a huge boulder. Somehow—I suspected it must be by maejic after Yallick hinted as much—it stayed dry inside, and the wind couldn't get in to put out the candles. Yallick used the shelter for his morning meditation, but had yielded it to me for the afternoons.

As the dry leaves on the path crunched beneath my feet, my thoughts turned to my older brother, Breyard. I hadn't been able to break the habit of worrying about him, not after spending a month trying to rescue him. Why had Yallick sent him away so soon—only a day after we'd arrived at his cottage? Why wouldn't Breyard explain what had happened to him? And what exactly *had* happened? He'd told Traz and me about what it had been like in that awful prison they'd kept him in, and about his sham trial. He even had some vague memories about the execution fight. But about what happened after Xyla, the dragon, had snatched him away, he wouldn't tell me any more. He just gave me a maddening smile and said, "All in good time." Then Yallick sent him away, home to our parents. And he'd seemed glad to go, almost as if he were grateful to escape.

When I reached the meditation shelter, I dragged my thoughts away from their pointless spiral and ducked inside.

A wooden seat, carved from a tree trunk, faced out, and in front of it stood a stone table. I sat down and looked at the bare trees interspersed here and there with evergreens.

In this quiet place, meditation was easy. I placed the meditation candles—blue and purple today, as it turned out—in holes in the surface of the table. After I lit them, light flickered on the rock above and around me, twinkling where it struck bits of mica.

I stared into the flames for a moment, then closed my eyes. One deep breath. Another. My mind's eye closed, leaving my imagination blank. I felt the vibration of the life of the forest surrounding me, and matched my heart's rhythm to it. The vibrations flowed through my body, which began to feel as if it had turned into something fluid. I swirled and spun round, celebrating the dance of life and my own place in it.

Eventually, the flow stopped and my eyelids fluttered open. The candlelight still flickered, the forest still surrounded me, and I still sat in the same seat as I had every afternoon since my return to Crowthorne. But power still surged within me as it never had before. I looked at my hands, half expecting to find them glowing, but they looked just as they always had, right down to a thin line of dirt under my fingernails that I never seemed to be able to get entirely clean.

I blew out the candles and took them with me when I returned to the cottage. Yallick, sitting at the table reading an ancient illustrated manuscript, looked up when I walked inside. He smiled.

"You did it," he said in his slightly raspy voice.

"Did what?" I asked.

He stood up and walked over to me, looking closely at my face. "You accessed the power." He touched my cheek with surprising gentleness. "You glow from it."

I looked at my hands again, confused. "No, I'm not." I showed him my hands. "See?"

He actually laughed. "No, no, not that kind of glow. But I can see it in your face. Come; sit down and tell me."

I did as he asked, still completely mystified as to what he was talking about. When I was done, he slapped the table with his hand, making the fruit in the wooden bowl jump.

"Yes! Your skills are markedly improving. I am quite proud of you, Donavah." I sat there, stunned. It was as if I were talking to my father instead of the maejic master who'd grudgingly agreed to teach me. "Off with you, now." Yallick shooed me away as if I were the cat. "Go check on Xyla."

"All right," I said, rising quickly. Anything to get away from his confusing behavior.

I set the candles on the table, intending to take them back to my room when I returned. Just before the door closed behind me, I heard Yallick mutter almost gleefully, "Ah, blue and purple. Blue and purple."

What could possibly be the significance of that, I wondered as I walked to the nearby clearing where Traz and I had, following Xyla's precise directions, created a bed of dead leaves and fresh-turned earth for her.

She now lay on her bed, her eyes closed. I shuffled my feet as I approached, not wanting to startle her. One eyelid opened a fraction. "Ah. Donavah." Xyla's voice spoke inside my head, and it was this ability to communicate with animals that was a mark of the gift of maejic. Not that this was necessarily a good thing, as practicing maejic had been outlawed in Alloway centuries before. That had not, of course, stopped the mages, but only forced them—us—into hiding.

I approached the huge red dragon and placed a hand on her jaw. Her skin was incredibly soft and smooth, and I loved touching her. "How are you, Xyla?"

"I am tired, but otherwise fine."

I scowled. "Still tired? You've done nothing but sleep since we got here." What could be wrong with her? She'd never been like this on our journey.

"I hunt, too. Do not worry about me; I am well."

I leaned against her shoulder, just absorbing her presence. Then I heard the crunching of footsteps approaching her other side. I was just about to ask who was there, when I heard Traz's voice.

"Hello, my lovely lady," he whispered, and I had to strain to hear. "I'm working hard. I'm getting stronger. I'm quite sure I'll be able to hear you soon."

I almost gasped in surprise. Did Traz mean he was trying to *become* maejic? Was that even possible? From what Yallick and Oleeda said, you were born with it, you didn't acquire it. And what happened to his desire to be a bard?

Then I wondered how I was going to get away without the boy discovering that I'd overheard his plan. Before I could figure out what to do, Traz walked around Xyla's head. He froze when he saw me standing there, and I'm sure I had a guilty expression on my face.

He spoke first. "You won't tell anyone, will you?"

For a moment I toyed with the idea of pretending that I didn't know what he was talking about, but I decided that wouldn't be fair.

I shook my head. "No, of course I won't. But why, Traz? Why would you want to?"

"What do you mean, why would I want to? I love Xyla, but I can't hear her. Everyone else, all the mages, they can. They all keep having conversations that I can't hear. How do you think that makes me feel?"

To tell the truth, I'd never thought about that, and I had to admit I could understand his point. "But, Traz, I can't hear other conversations, either." He gave me an exasperated look. "I know, I know. That doesn't make up for it. Still, why would you want to become maejic? You don't want always to live in hiding like this, do you?"

He stuck out his jaw stubbornly. "I'll do it. You just wait and see if I don't."

✦

I sit and ponder the setback we've endured. A red dragon—red!—in our grasp. Yet she slipped through our fingers when we least expected it.

No matter. My son has done his work well, and our original plan proceeds apace. The red dragon was nothing more than an aside, and her loss signifies nothing of importance. Success shall be ours, with or without her, for the plan was set in motion five hundred long years ago. We have played the game carefully, and victory is at hand.

Tomorrow—yes, tomorrow!—I send forth the messages that will move the final pieces into position. Once the last play has begun, no one will be able to keep us from Securing the Queen's Heart. Ah, such a game of Talisman and Queen it has been! I shall savor the glory of the king's final defeat.

two

I arrived back at the cottage just as Oleeda was getting ready to leave. A master at Roylinn Academy, where I'd been studying magic, she was also—unbeknownst to the authorities, of course—a mage. It was she who had sent me to Yallick and she who'd convinced him to take over my tuition.

She took my hands and gave me a peck on my cheek. As she let go, I realized with a start that there had been no shock of vibration.

"How'd you do that?" I asked.

"Do what?"

"The, umm, well, when we touched. It was like normal, not like that first time."

"Ah, that. You will learn how to control it. It only takes training." She smiled in a very unsatisfying sort of way. "I must return to the academy now, or they will begin to wonder what has become of me. Have you any messages for your friends?"

I thought of Marileesa, who must be already practicing for singing at the Summer Solstice celebration, and of Loreen, who was probably broken-hearted over Breyard's disappearance. Well, I couldn't tell them anything without telling them everything, so I just shook my head. "Just give them my love and tell them I miss them." I sighed. "I don't even know when I'll see them again."

Oleeda gave me a sympathetic look. "I know it is hard to be so far from everyone and everything you know. It will not always be this way. Be patient."

"But why?" The words burst out of me unexpectedly. Yallick would've given me one of his disapproving scowls, but Oleeda placed a gentle hand on my shoulder. I continued. "What is all this being patient about? I've been here for weeks and haven't done anything."

Oleeda smiled again. "You have not 'done nothing.' It might seem like nothing to you because it is on your own insides. But those of us watching on the outside, we can see you growing."

I had to restrain myself from rolling my eyes. She sounded like Mama. But even while that was annoying, it was also comforting. And now she was leaving, and I'd be stuck here with Yallick, who definitely was *not* like Papa. Well, not often, anyway.

Oleeda kissed my cheek again. "Well, if you have no messages, it is time for me to be off."

Traz jogged up just then. "You have my letter to Mama?"

"Of course I do. Tucked safely in the bottom of my pack."

"Your mother knows you're here?" I asked in surprise.

He looked at me as if I'd just said the stupidest thing he'd heard all day. "Of course she knows. How else do you think I could stay?"

Oleeda placed a hand on my shoulder. "Not all non-maejic folk oppose us," she said. "She was relieved to learn Traz was safe, and saw the wisdom of him not returning to the academy, not for a while yet."

"Never is more likely," said Traz.

Oleeda smiled. "We shall see. Goodbye, and take care of yourselves until I see you again."

We walked out with her and watched her mount her horse. With a final wave, she was gone. Just as Breyard was gone. What was it that kept making everyone leave?

+ + +

That evening, I sat in the front room with Yallick. It had turned quite cold when the sun set, and the heat of the fire made me feel comfortable, almost drowsy. We were supposed to be having a lesson, but Yallick just sat staring into the flames. Finally, he broke the silence.

"Did Xyla sleep this much on your journey?"

I was startled to hear him voice one of my own concerns. "No. Well, no, I can't say that." I thought back. "She stayed hidden during the day while we went into the cities. Then she got captured. So I don't actually know. Maybe she did sleep a lot."

"Hmm," Yallick said, frowning. My heart started beating faster. Yallick being worried had to be a bad sign. On the other hand, what did he really know about dragons? What, for that matter, did *I* know? "We will need to keep watch on her. Maybe it is nothing but an old man's needless worrying." He gave me a small smile. "So. I wish to speak with you about your afternoon meditation session. Tell me again what happened."

I'd been studying with Yallick for only a few weeks, but one thing I'd quickly learned was that he didn't have much patience with drawn-out explanations. Besides, I didn't know what he was after. I kept it short and simple. "I took the blue and purple candles." He nodded. "I went to the shelter under the rock. When I started meditating, it took almost no time to find my calm center, and suddenly I felt," I paused as I tried to think of the right way to put it, "I felt as if I'd joined the dance of life."

Yallick closed his eyes, his face expressionless, took a deep breath, and let it out again. "Yes. Yes. Do you know what is happening, and why?"

I thought a moment more. "No. I don't actually understand any of it. But I *think* it has something to do with mixing the candles."

Yallick's eyes flew open. "Indeed. It has everything to do with mixing the candles. What exactly did they teach you about meditation at that school of yours?" He waved a hand as if dismissing Roylinn.

"Well, each year is divided into four seasons, of course, and each season is divided into twelve weeks. There are different candleholders for each season, and a different color candle for each week, repeated in the same order each season."

"Yes, yes," snapped Yallick, watching me closely now, his startling eyes boring into mine. "I know all that. But did they teach you why?"

I didn't understand what he was trying to find out, so I just said the first thing I thought of. "The colors of the candles represent qualities to enhance life."

A long pause. "Donavah, you are nothing if not a diligent student." Something in his tone of voice told me he didn't exactly mean this as a compliment. "You are clearly quite capable of learning what is set before you and repeating it back. But my question to you is 'why?' Why are the colors assigned to certain weeks? Why are they not mixed? Why does there need to be any sort of order at all? Why?"

"I don't know," I said simply.

Yallick clapped his hands together once, leaning forward. "Exactly! You do not know. And you do not know because they do not tell you. They do not want you to know." He shrugged. "Or maybe they do not know themselves." He leaned back in his chair. "Relax, my girl, and I will tell you why.

"You see, back in the deeps of time, maejic was recognized as the superior art. There were, of course, many who could aspire only to the lower spells and did not have the full gift. They called their lesser art *magic*."

"I know all this. Oleeda explained it to me."

"Do not interrupt me, girl!" Yallick's eyes blazed, and I dipped my head slightly in apology. Then he continued. "The foundation of maejic's power is in self-control—something which *you* need to acquire—and self-control is strengthened in meditation. Are you familiar with the formulas used in the making of meditation candles?"

"No. I only know the colors and their properties."

Yallick snorted. "That should not surprise me. Well, each color of candle is made with a slightly different blend of herbs, thus each gives off a different aroma when burned. It is the aroma that strengthens the spirit for its work.

"And it is that which the magicians of yore could not abide. The candles are at their weakest when two of the same color are burned together. The magicians, despising a power that they did not—could not—share, strove to weaken the power of the candles by creating a new tradition that they could not be mixed. That tradition is now observed as incontrovertible law."

"So," I began tentatively, then continued when Yallick didn't stop me, "what they teach us to be right and proper is really the exact wrong way."

"Indeed. I think you have experienced this yourself, most especially today."

I thought for a moment. "So is there a chart I can study to learn the best way to mix candles?"

Yallick threw his head back and laughed. "No, my dear. This is something you must learn for yourself. Experience, not study, will teach you how to harness power."

Harness power. Those words struck a chord within me. It was all well and good to be able to cast magic spells, but the power I'd felt in my meditation session—that kind of power would strengthen me to . . . to . . . to do anything. I relaxed in my chair, letting the heat of the fire wash over me.

After a while, Yallick spoke again in a soft voice. "Magic is actually quite simplistic. It takes the energy all around us and re-channels it. Granted, not an insignificant skill, when you think about it." He pointed to a basket of ripe summer fruit sitting on the mantle. "It can be very useful. But maejic is so much more. It . . . can you guess?"

"It . . . it . . . creates power?"

"Not quite." Yallick smiled. "Creating power, that would be quite a feat, would it not? No, maejic does not create power but gathers it and concentrates it. Like what you did with the locked door in the arena."

I looked at him in surprise. "I didn't do anything. It wasn't locked."

"Donavah, you do not actually believe that an unguarded entrance to the arena would be left unlocked, do you?" He shook his head and waggled a finger at me. "The king makes quite a lot of money selling tickets. I might not have been there, but I assure you, that door was locked."

"But, like I said, I didn't do anything."

"You *think* you did nothing. What were you doing just before you opened the door?"

"I was . . ." I sucked in my breath. "I was meditating."

"And a moment later, when you desperately needed the door to open, it did. That, my apprentice, is maejic." Yallick smiled.

+ + +

I suppose I should have expected it. The next morning's meditation session went as badly as it possibly could. I closed my eyes and rummaged in my desk drawer to pull out two candles at random. Orange for creativity and yellow for kindness. I sat on my prayer mat in my small room, stuck the candles into some ancient holders, carved from petrified wood, that Yallick had given me, lit the candles, and waited to see what the power would feel like today. And waited. And waited.

I told myself that trying to force something is usually the best way to hinder it. Then I tried to find my calm center. It was gone, almost as if it had never existed. Was yesterday's taste all that I would ever experience for myself?

Finally, I gave up and blew out the candles. Someone knocked on my door, and Traz called my name softly. It was uncanny how he always seemed to know right when I finished meditating.

"Come," I said, and he opened the door, breathless from running, as usual.

"It's weird outside," he said, sitting on my cot and placing his staff across his lap.

"Weird how?"

"I don't know. It's ice cold, there's no wind, and there's almost no sound at all. Almost like the forest is holding its breath in anticipation."

I looked at Traz, wondering when he'd become so fanciful. He was usually the more practical one of us. "In anticipation of what?"

He shrugged. "Dunno. But it's weird."

"Well, come on. I need to get ready for a lesson with Yallick."

"I'm sure glad I don't have to study with him. He's always in such a bad mood."

"A lot, but not always," I said as we walked into the front room of the cottage.

Just then there came a loud pounding on the door. "Yallick! Yallick!" The door opened and someone burst into the room along with a blast of cold air from outside.

"Anazian!" Traz cried in surprise. "What's wrong?"

I looked at the mage with whom Traz was staying. His eyes darted all around the room, although a quick glance was all that was needed to see that Yallick wasn't there. Anazian's face was paler than usual, and it looked as if he'd left his own cottage without even combing his hair—which was quite unusual for him. And strangest of all, his hands fluttered all about, as if he didn't know what to do with them. All in all, he didn't look anything like the composed, handsome man I knew him to be.

"Yallick hasn't returned from his morning meditation yet," I said, taking a step toward the open door to close it.

"Yes, I have," Yallick said, striding through the doorway, gripping his meditation candles in his hand. In a moment of strange clarity, I saw that his knuckles were white. "What is it, Anazian?"

"They're coming, sir. They march against us!"

"Who?" Traz, Yallick, and I all said together.

"The king's men." He swallowed, and his Adam's apple bobbed. "The Royal Guard."

✦

Ah, Arellia. My sweet Arellia. Wife of my youth, mother of my beloved son. I miss you still, though many long years have passed since our final parting. I taste your sweet breath; I feel your soft hair. There has been no other but you.

I am powerful, far beyond our hopes and dreams. But the flavor of victory is bittersweet without you by my side. I will miss you until I draw my last breath.

If my power could bring you back to me, I would spend it all. But there is no magic that can stretch beyond the grave.

It may yet be long ere I join you, but be patient. Await me, my love, in Otherworld.

†HREE

We all froze. Yallick was the first to move, and he closed the door. Then he grabbed Anazian's upper arms and stared into his eyes.

His next words came out like a hiss between his clenched teeth. "What do you mean? How soon?"

Anazian licked his lips. I couldn't blame him. If Yallick had been looking at me like that, I would have wanted the ground to open up and swallow me.

"I don't know, sir. I just received a message bird from my cousin. She says they passed through her village yesterday. That would put them here in less than a week."

Yallick released Anazian and started pacing. "How could they know we are here?" he eventually muttered to himself. "This community has remained hidden for a thousand years and more. It is impossible that they have discovered us." Several more laps around the room, the only noise the crackling of the fire and the beating of my heart.

I'd just spent several weeks on the run from the Royal Guard. Only being able to fly on Xyla had saved me. But Xyla couldn't save the whole community of mages; there were hundreds of them living scattered all around the woods.

Finally Yallick spoke again. "We must call a council. Anazian, how many birds have you at the ready?"

Anazian stood straighter, calmer, as if Yallick's assumption of responsibility removed a burden from him. "Eight, sir. Maybe ten."

"All right. Here is what we shall do."

Ten minutes later, I raced along a path toward Ranna's cottage whilst Traz went in the other direction to Klemma's, with word that Yallick was calling an emergency council for midday. Anazian's birds would carry messages to the other council members, some of whom would be hard-pressed to arrive in time for the start of the meeting, even on horseback.

When I reached Ranna's door, I pounded on it, just as Anazian had on Yallick's only minutes, it seemed, before. "Ranna!" I cried, "Ranna!" Where could she be? Why didn't she answer the door? I hammered again. "Ranna!"

"What, my child?" She appeared from around a corner of the cottage. Her hands were coated with earth and held a basket of potatoes. There was a large smudge of dirt on her forehead. "What is your panic?"

"The king," I said, running over to her. "He's marching against us."

"The king himself?" The doubt in Ranna's eyes was apparent, even to me.

"I don't know," I snapped, and she stepped back at my vehemence, frowning. "Maybe not himself. But the Royal Guard."

Something in my voice or face must have convinced her that I wasn't joking, for she looked at me closely. "How do you know this?"

"Anazian received word from his cousin or something like that. Yallick has called a council at midday. Anazian's birds are taking messages to the others. Oh, please, Ranna, hurry!"

She looked deep into my eyes, and I could almost feel her rooting around in my thoughts. Then she nodded. "Tell Yallick I will be there."

"All right." I fled before she could ask me any more questions I couldn't answer.

When I got back to Yallick's, I found him sitting in front of the fire, staring at a book on his lap. The fingertips of one hand gently stroked the cover, almost as if the book were a living thing.

"Ah, Donavah," he said as I hung my cloak on its peg. "Come here, please."

I walked over, unable to take my eyes from the book, which seemed to glow in the firelight.

"I had meant to wait, but now there is a new sense of urgency. Sit, girl, sit."

I did, wondering how he could be so calm, as if nothing were happening.

"This book, it is a maejic treasure. It has been in my keeping since I was elected to this position. I do not know if I am right, but I deem that now is the time to bring it into the open. It concerns you, or rather, your companion yonder." He nodded his head in the general direction of Xyla. "For now, just read it."

He handed it to me, and I accepted it reverently. Something about it—perhaps the musty odor given off by the vellum pages, perhaps the way the colors of the illustration on the cover seemed to leap into life—made this a solemn moment.

"Go to your room, now. I will call you when I want you."
He gave me a small, encouraging smile, then stared into the
fire.

I carried the book to my room and set it gently on my
writing desk. A beam of sunlight fell on it, and as if it had
been waiting for that very thing, a red dragon practically
leapt off the cover. I gasped. And sat down quickly.

Yes, there in the whorls of gold, blue, and green flew an
unmistakably red dragon. And it breathed fire! How had I
not seen it right away?

With great care, I opened the book. The hand-scribed
text was in a script I couldn't read. Yallick knew that, and
yet he wanted me to study it anyway. How curious. But the
pictures!

In the first one, a copper-colored adult dragon sat gazing
into the sky in which ten or so small red dragons flew. The
second illustration showed a group of red dragons sitting in a
circle, as if in council.

As I looked at the second picture, a movement from the
first one caught the corner of my eye. When I looked at it
directly, it was exactly the same as it had been before. But
when I turned my head a little and didn't look quite straight
at it, the picture seemed to come alive! The young dragons
cavorted, swooping and soaring, while their mother bugled
at them in good humor. I could almost *hear* her!

As I watched, scarcely able to breathe in the excitement of
my discovery, all the pictures began to move, and soon I'd pieced
together the story they told. It didn't matter that I couldn't read
the accompanying text—the pictures told their own tale.

The copper matriarch, Xylera, brought forth eleven red dragons, the like of which had never been seen before in all the world. Her mate, the silver dragon Qonth, ruled Alloway together with King Gren. Qonth decided not to tell Gren of the surprising brood his offspring turned out to be. Instead, he sent Xylera and their young into the mountains, that humans would not learn of them. Together, Qonth and Xylera breathed power and knowledge into their progeny, desiring that in some future day, their descendants would wrest ruling power away from the humans.

The last picture showed a large formation of fire-breathing dragons sweeping down into battle.

My breath caught in my throat as I looked away from the book. That must have been the battle where they were overcome. I knew that story. Yallick seemed to think that it was linked to Xyla—and to me—here and now. So that's why he wanted me to study this book. I ran my fingers lightly over the images, feeling the texture of the ink and gold leaf.

I began to turn the page, eager to see the next story, when Yallick called to me.

"Donavah, I need you to go check on Xyla."

As I walked past the group gathered in the main room, Yallick caught my eye, and a pulse of understanding shot through me. He needed for me to be outside, out of earshot of the council. I frowned. After everything I'd already been through, everything I'd done, when would I be old enough to participate?

I found the dragon sleeping yet again. The thin sunlight shone on her, although it didn't seem to actually warm the air much. Well, it was going to get colder before it got warmer. I pulled my cloak more tightly around me.

For a little while, I just stood and looked at Xyla. I still hadn't gotten used to the idea that this breathtaking animal was my friend. She was the only known red dragon; the rest were white, silver, gold, copper—colors like that.

The story was that the dragonmasters in Ultria had been trying to develop new hybrids, and the Ultrian Prince, Havden, had sent an egg from one of the clutches to Princess Rycina, the king of Alloway's eldest daughter, as a gift to celebrate their betrothal. En route, the egg had been stolen, and by a very strange set of circumstances, ended up in my brother Breyard's possession, whereupon it hatched. Breyard released the baby dragon into the woods near Roylinn, the magic academy where we were both students, but the egg had been traced and Breyard arrested. I knew he hadn't stolen the egg, but he was tried and convicted anyway, and sentenced to death in the king's dragon-fighting pits.

I gave a little half-smile. If I hadn't gone after him to try—foolishly and unsuccessfully—to prove him innocent, he would be dead now. For that little baby dragon, Xyla, had gone to Stychs—a mysterious place out of the world entirely—to grow, then flown Traz and me to the capital city, Penwick. Unfortunately, she'd been spotted and captured. Apparently thrilled to have acquired a new, unique, full-grown dragon, the king had decided to pit her against the biggest criminal in the land, egg-thief Breyard. As the "fight" began, Traz's magic staff had broken the net of spells covering the arena. Xyla seized Breyard and disappeared—to Stychs as

I learned later—and came back for Traz and me, and flew us all to safety.

"You worry." Xyla's voice intruded on my thoughts. I hadn't noticed her eyes open. Now she was watching me.

"Yes, I *am* worried." I walked over and leaned against her. For the first time, it occurred to me that she could swallow me whole if she were so inclined. I'd seen that just about happen in the one fight I'd watched between a dragon and a man. I instantly tried to blot that image from my mind, before Xyla could pick it up. No point in distressing her.

"You worry too much. What is wrong now?"

I knew I shouldn't tell her, but I really couldn't hide it from her. "The king's men are coming. I'm afraid they're going to attack." I took a breath to try to steady myself and keep from breaking into a panic. "Oh, Xyla, the Royal Guard are coming after me again. Why can't I just be left in peace? Why is everyone always hunting me down?"

I could almost hear her mental sigh. "It is not you they seek. And we are safe. They cannot find us here."

"How can you be so sure? Even Yallick is worried; he's called the council together."

"Then they shall decide what is to be done. There is nothing for you to worry about."

"That's easy for you to say. You don't have Yallick trying to drive all kinds of knowledge into your head." Which wasn't quite true or fair, but the thought of seeing the Royal Guard in their purple and scarlet uniforms sent shivers down my spine. Once I'd thought they looked handsome; now just a glimpse of those colors terrified me. And made me say things I didn't really mean.

"I thought you wished to learn from Yallick," Xyla said, her voice sounding a little confused.

"Oh, I do. I guess. It's just that . . ." What exactly was it that was bothering me? "He seems to think," I said slowly, trying to put my vague feelings into words, "that there's something special about me, as if there's a task I have to do. I mean, I'm just me. What special thing could I ever do?"

"No one knows what they can do until they have to do it. You know that. And you have already done something special. Because of you, Breyard is still alive."

I sighed. "Yeah, that's true. But still, I wish Yallick wasn't so . . . so . . . intense. He kind of scares me sometimes."

"Yallick is a good man."

I snorted. "He might be a good man, but he isn't always a nice one."

"He has had . . . disappointments."

There was, quite simply, nothing I could say in reply to that. I decided instead to try to return to the original topic of conversation.

"I'm afraid we're going to have to leave here."

"But where would we go?" Xyla seemed honestly perplexed.

"I don't know. But Xyla, if the Royal Guard try to capture you, promise me something, won't you?"

"What?"

"Promise that you'll get away. Go back to Stychs if that's the only way to escape. Please."

"Donavah, I cannot go to Stychs."

"Why ever not? I mean, if that's what you have to do. It's better than getting recaptured."

"I cannot go to Stychs," she repeated. "I am pregnant."

✦

I watch her and wonder: what could have been were I not too old, were she not too young. It is not that I never wished to marry. No, only that I never found the right woman with whom to wed and to bear my seed.

The rearing of children is hard—hard and unpredictable—and I do not believe that I regret having escaped the trouble of it. And yet . . . and yet.

Donavah is mine neither to wed nor to rear. Rather, it seems to be meant that I am to teach her, teach her well and truly, so that she can fulfill her destiny.

This is not an insignificant task. Indeed, it will surely effect a change on the entire world order.

I accept my fate.

Four

✦

I burst into Yallick's cottage, and the group of mages turned and stared at me. The man who'd been speaking still had his mouth open, although no words came out. Anger kindled in Yallick's eyes, but I spoke before he could.

"Xyla is pregnant!" I announced to my stunned audience. I was panting from my mad dash, and I tried to get my breath. "Sorry to interrupt, but I knew you needed to know."

Everyone, including me, looked at Yallick. His eyes had become slightly unfocused, as if he were concentrating on something. The only sounds were the snapping of the flames in the fireplace and my breathing. I closed my mouth and tried to breathe more quietly.

After several moments, Yallick's attention returned to the group in front of him.

"This explains it," he said. "Why she has been sleeping so much. And, of course, it does affect our plans." His gaze turned to me. "You may go now, Donavah." A hint of a smile appeared. "Thank you for bringing this news."

I went back outside, wondering what to do with myself. I mentally reached for Xyla, but I could tell she was trying to get back to sleep, so I left her alone. A gust of cold wind blew past, and I shivered. I knew just the place to go: the meditation shelter. I would be snug there, even without a fire to keep me warm.

When I arrived at the shelter, I took a few moments to take a really good look at it, as if etching it on my memory. Only a few weeks ago, I didn't know of its existence, but now I felt as if it were an old friend I was leaving behind forever. Even though Yallick hadn't suggested it within my hearing, I was certain that we would be going away. A current of sad farewell pulsed through the woods all around me. Maybe that's what Traz had felt when he described it as being weird outside.

I placed a hand on the granite boulder. The surface was rough and hard and . . . warm! How could that be? Surely even the most magic of objects couldn't generate their own heat on a cold day? I walked around the boulder to the opening and ducked inside, where it was as toasty warm as if a huge fire were burning in a tiny room. First I opened my cloak, then took it off entirely.

I sat on the seat and closed my eyes. Power whorled around me, and it had a distinct masculine feel. I tried to focus on it, to discover what it was. I seemed to perceive colors, even with eyes closed: purple, midnight blue, deep forest green.

Without thinking what I was doing or why, I reached out a hand as if to catch a falling feather. Something tickled my palm. I concentrated on the sensation, trying to draw more of it to myself. I imagined power spooling into my palm like a ball of yarn winding itself up.

When I opened my eyes to see if there really was anything there at all, I saw in my hand the image of a head: Yallick's! It began to fade at my startled gasp, so I concentrated harder.

The image grew stronger. Yallick's eyes were closed, and his lips moved ever so slightly, as if he were whispering to himself. Free to gaze at him without having to worry about his sharp tongue reprimanding me, I looked at him more closely than ever before.

He had a strong jawline that jutted out almost in arrogance—almost, but not quite. His long, white-blond hair swept back from a high forehead. The wrinkles around his eyes and mouth didn't show, and he looked much younger than he actually was.

Then his lips stopped moving. His blue-green eyes opened, and from them, a beam of light shot past my shoulder. I cried out in guilty surprise and moved as if to drop the image, which instantly disappeared.

I looked around, wondering what had just happened. The warmth was quickly dissipating, and I pulled my cloak back on, shivering more in reaction to what had just happened than with cold.

The shelter now felt strange and unfamiliar. I didn't understand how I'd conjured that image. Had I done it at all, or was it something else? It had felt more like I was gathering strands of power. But how—and why—had it turned into Yallick's image?

I stepped back into the cold air and decided to take a walk. Following a path that lead the opposite direction from Yallick's cottage, I walked quickly to keep warm. Dead leaves crunched underfoot, and every once in awhile I saw a forest creature scurry across the path or up a tree. Birds flitted amongst the branches, and I wondered how much longer it would be before they finally headed south to warmer climes.

Eventually I crossed another path leading more or less back toward Yallick's, so I took it. This was a new path to me, one I hadn't explored in the weeks since we'd arrived here. At first, it was a wide track, even open to the sky overhead, but before long, the trees drew closer. The path began to wind, and even though it was nearing midday and there wasn't a cloud in the sky, the light grew dim.

I began to feel an unfamiliar vibration in the air. It was dark, and old, and wild. I stopped walking and tried to discern where it was coming from. There. A little way from the path, there was a patch of—well, it wasn't exactly darkness—more like a blurry patch, where the shapes of the trees were fuzzy.

I closed my eyes. The vibration had frightened me a little at first, not because it was threatening but because it was so strange; now it seemed to be drawing me to its source. Eyes still closed, I followed it. A piece of my rational mind warned me that I was surely going to crash into a tree, but I pushed the thought down and obeyed what seemed to be instinct. And I didn't misstep.

Then I stopped, as if at an unspoken command. The air crackled, dancing around me and making my skin tingle. I smiled. The sounds of the life of the forest around me became magnified. The twittering of birds echoed loudly, and the scuttling of small creatures was more like a herd of wild horses crashing through the trees. An incessant clickety-clacking was the sound of insects gnawing and marching their way through the nearby trees.

Even before I opened my eyes, I knew that I must be in the middle of the grey patch I'd seen. Finally, I looked around.

I stood in the center of a circle of stones. Not huge boulders, but small ones, small enough for me to sit on. Only one rose higher than my knees.

The ground inside the circle was soft loam, and I thought I could see the footprints of bare human feet here and there. Bare feet? In this weather? They must be recent or else the rain several days ago would have washed them away.

The trees were hoary and grey, with strands of lichen trailing off the branches like ancient beards.

The vibrations began to pulse, and I could almost hear the music of the stars. I began to walk around the circle, and before I quite realized what was happening, I found I was dancing. My feet traced an intricate pattern, and I swirled and whirled and sprang spinning into the air. Round and round the circle I sped, feeling almost as if I could fly. I leapt from stone to stone, defying gravity itself. The stars smiled down on me.

"Donavah!" Yallick's gravelly voice stopped me in my tracks. He raised a hand, palm facing me. The energy all around me stilled. "It has taken me forever to find you. Come now." His words were curt, but I felt no hint of anger in them. And his piercing gaze, while intense and almost curious, didn't scare me as it so often did. "Come."

I took a few steps before it struck me that it had grown dark.

We walked at first in silence. I kept waiting for Yallick to tear into me for being undisciplined and out of control, but he didn't. Instead, he strode along at a comfortable pace, as if it were our usual habit to take a moonlit stroll through the woods.

Eventually I stopped feeling awkward and told him about what had happened in the meditation shelter. He gave me a strange look, narrowing his eyes, then, as he so often had done before, asked me to tell him everything again. As I did, I tried to repeat word for word what I'd said the first time, but I quickly noticed that I kept saying things slightly differently. Like "threads" the first time and "strands" the second. Was it these tiny differences that helped him understand more clearly what I was trying to say? I stopped putting so much effort into my narrative and just let the words flow.

By the time I'd been all the way through the story for the second time, we reached a stream not far from the cottage. With his long legs, Yallick leaped across. I used the stepping stones since I didn't want to risk getting wet. As I reached the other side, Yallick held out his hand to help me up the bank. With a sudden and inexplicable feeling of disdain, I spurned his offer of assistance. He just shrugged and gave me an infuriating cockeyed grin.

"So what do you think it all means?" I asked as we resumed our walk.

"What do *you* think it means?" Before I could deliver the sarcastic retort that rose to my lips, he raised a hand as if to stop me. "I want you to think about it for a moment and try to formulate your own conclusion. Then we will consider it. Thus you will better learn how to judge things."

I thought about it. "Well, there was definitely power there. I could feel it on my skin."

"Good. What kind of power?"

I thought some more. "Something to do with . . ." I hesitated because it seemed so stupid, then went on. "Something to do with you."

"Indeed. Because it was me that you saw?"

I nodded. "But I don't understand why. You were meeting with the rest of the council; you weren't nearby. And you couldn't possibly have been thinking of me."

"Perhaps not, although you should not be so quick to assume to know what people are thinking."

I looked at him, but he was staring off into the distance as we walked. For a moment, I wondered how much attention he was really paying to this conversation.

"What else?" he finally asked.

I pondered, but couldn't think of anything more to say.

"You cannot think of any reason why you might have felt power in the shelter?" When I didn't answer, he continued. "In the place where I had been meditating not long before?"

Then it seemed so obvious I wanted to melt in embarrassment. I fell back a step or two, and Yallick turned to look at me. "What?" he asked in a sharp tone of voice.

"You make it sound so simple," I muttered.

He stopped and made me stop, too. He stood facing me and took both of my hands in his. "Donavah," and his voice was as gentle as I'd ever heard it. "Many things sound simple once you figure them out. But nothing is ever as simple as it seems. You have made great progress. To even sense the residue of my meditation—half the mages here could not do that. To shape that residue into my image . . ." He trailed off and sighed. He released one of my hands and tucked the other one into the crook of his arm, then started walking slowly again.

I didn't know quite what to make of all this, so I walked along at his side wordlessly. After a few strides, we fell into step, and I began to feel more comfortable than I ever would have expected in Yallick's presence.

He didn't speak again until we reached the cottage. He paused as we entered the clearing, and I disengaged my hand from his arm. "I need to ask you for a favor before you retire for the night. I need you to help me move something."

"Sure. What?"

The moonlight shone full on his face as he looked at me, and his eyes glinted as he said, "That."

I looked where he was pointing. "You've got to be kidding!" I squealed as I realized he meant the house-sized boulder behind his cottage.

The power of maejic never ceases to awe me. That we must keep its use secret is criminal. How many people have gone to their graves never knowing they had the gift—or knowing, choosing not to use it?

Our numbers decrease. There are scarcely enough of us left to maintain the balance of power. We weary and are in danger of growing weak.

Long have I pondered what it will take to put things to rights. Maejic was outlawed when the dragons were overthrown from joint rule. Will it be restored when they regain their rightful place? Is Xyla the precursor? I am tempted to pin my hopes on her, but this does not seem wise, for many things can yet go wrong.

Though go we to rest now,
Say not thou "defeat."
The power of ages
Again shall be meet.

Ascent from the ashes,
Descent from the stars,
The power of ages
Once more shall be ours.

A strong one will quicken
And harvest alone
The power of ages
To lead us all home.

Is Xyla the strong one? Is Donavah?

FIVE

"I assure you I am not kidding." Yallick's chuckle made me look back at him. "Come inside," he said.

I followed him into the cottage, the inside of which looked nothing at all as it had when I'd left it earlier in the day. The furniture was pushed back against the walls, the rugs were rolled up leaving the floor bare, and not a single book, manuscript, or instrument was to be seen anywhere.

"I was right," I burst out. "We *are* leaving."

"Yes, indeed. And who knows when or even if we shall return?" I detected a wistful note in his voice. "What we cannot carry on our backs we must leave behind."

"But if the king's men are coming . . . what about all your things?"

"That is what I need your help with. I have already buried everything of import—"

"Buried your books?" I interrupted. "They'll all be ruined!"

Yallick snorted. "I think not. I would have hoped you would trust me to do better than that. Everything is safely sealed in magic trunks. But even the most junior of Roylinn's novices could open the trunks if they were found. That is why I need your help. We must move that boulder to cover the spot where the trunks are buried."

I looked at him as if he were crazy, and then it dawned on me. Of course! We would move the boulder using our power. My eyes widened. "I've never . . . I can't . . ." I spluttered. Then I rose to the challenge in Yallick's eyes. "All right. Teach me what to do." He smiled in satisfaction.

He led the way back outside and around to the back. The boulder was at least twenty feet across and close to half that high.

"Close your eyes and compose your thoughts." Yallick's voice was soft, almost chanting.

I took another look at the huge rock, then did as I was told.

"Gather your power."

I took a deep breath and raised my hands, as if feeling for the threads, the strands of power to weave into substance. There—on my fingertips, now in my palms. I gathered it as Yallick instructed.

"Direct it to the boulder."

I sent the ropes of power to surround it, lift it into the air. Not much, just a few inches. I heard the tiniest of gasps from my teacher, which I put out of my mind.

"Move it to the left, not far, maybe eight feet."

I felt like laughing, this was so easy. Obviously, Yallick was doing most of the work. Still, I was learning a new skill. With a slow movement of my hand, I slid the power to the left.

"By all the . . . !" Traz's voice rang through the night, shattering my concentration. The ground shuddered as the boulder fell. I almost lost my balance, but Yallick grabbed my arm. Traz sauntered over to us. From the look in Yallick's eyes, I knew the boy was in for a tongue-lashing. "That was awesome, Donavah!" Traz went on. "I didn't know you could do that. C'mon. Do it again!"

I braced myself for the expected torrent of anger from the mage, but before it came, the entire world seemed to tilt. Yallick caught me up in his arms before I fell, then quickly strode to the cottage. I tried to protest that I could walk, but no words came out. He carried me inside and to my room, placed me gently on my cot, and pulled several heavy blankets over me. I caught sight of Traz's worried face watching from the doorway, but I couldn't move. Panic started to seep into my stomach.

Yallick placed a warm hand on my forehead. "You are all right. Sleep now. We must leave before dawn." And I immediately fell asleep.

✦ ✦ ✦

I was softly prodded from a dreamless slumber to find Yallick looking down at me in the candlelight. "Awake?" he asked.

I nodded and pushed myself into a sitting position. I felt a little groggy, but nothing a cup of strong tea wouldn't take care of.

Yallick sat on the edge of the cot, and I moved my legs aside to give him more room.

"It is almost time to depart. But before we go, I must beg your forgiveness. What I did last night was utterly inexcusable."

"What do you mean? I don't understand. So I helped you move—"

"Helped me?" he interrupted. "Helped me? My dear, you did it all yourself."

I almost asked if he was kidding, but I could see the concern—concern for *me*—in his eyes.

"I did not think you would be able to do it; you have not yet had sufficient training. But after yesterday's events, it was wrong of me to put you to that kind of test. My only defense is that I did not expect you to succeed. But you did."

He paused, as if to let that sink in.

My voice came out in a whisper. "I . . . I did it all myself? That's not possible."

Yallick smiled. "I was surprised myself, despite my confidence in your abilities." He patted my shoulder. "It is almost time to leave. Traz has prepared porridge and tea. You must eat well, and then we will be off."

I rubbed the sleep out of my eyes. "But I haven't packed yet."

"Not to worry. Traz and I took care of that last night. Your pack is in the front room. Hurry along now." And he was gone, closing the door behind him.

I looked around the room. Although it was at least twice as big as my cell back at Roylinn Academy, I hadn't been here long enough to really make it mine. I'd set a few pinecones on the desk, but that was about it. Still, the bed was comfortable, and the thought of camping in the outdoors during Winter didn't make it seem less so. I sighed and threw back the covers, discovering with relief that I was still dressed in yesterday's clothes.

Breakfast improved my mood still more, so that when we left the cottage, I felt ready to face whatever was ahead. We hoisted our packs and went outside.

"Don't you want to lock the door?" I asked Yallick as we walked down the front path.

"*If* they find the place, a lock would scarcely slow them down."

Something about the way he stressed the word *if* made me look back. Sure enough, where the cottage had stood was now a meadowy glade. Even the boulder I'd moved the night before was gone.

"Then why did you have me move it?" I asked in exasperation.

"Because I have no idea whether they will be able to break the illusion. And even if they do not, the illusion will not last forever. Let us carry on."

Yallick took the lead, and Traz and I walked side by side behind him. We headed north.

The sky was just turning rosy in the dawn light when the mage Anazian joined us. He had a very serious look on his face, and he spoke with Yallick in a language I didn't understand. Not liking the feel of being left out, I slowed my steps to let the two men get a little ahead. Traz stayed with me.

"Where is Xyla?" I asked. "I didn't see her anywhere. I can't hear her, either."

Traz's winced a bit, reminding me of his secret wish to become maejic. "Yallick sent her ahead last night. Said she needs to travel when it's dark."

"But where'd she go?"

"To wherever we're supposed to camp tonight. I guess that's the plan for awhile, until we have to start traveling at night, too."

"At night?" I exclaimed much louder than I'd meant to. Anazian looked back at me. I smiled at him, and he turned back to Yallick. "At night?" I repeated more quietly. "You're joking."

Traz shrugged. "I'm not. And I can't imagine Yallick ever joking."

"You've got a point there," I agreed. Then I shivered. "It's already too cold to be outside at night."

"I know. And I think we're heading for the mountains on the northeast border."

"Great. Just great." I hunched up in my cloak, shoved my gloved hands deeper into my pockets, and trudged along in silence for awhile. I tried to enjoy the scenery, but the woods had suddenly lost their appeal.

+ + +

As the day progressed, more and more mages joined us, until we were a group of well over a hundred. Traz attached himself to Klemma, and I couldn't help smiling when I realized he'd managed to coax her into a verbal lesson on weaponry.

After lunch, Anazian joined me. "So, Donavah, how goes the teaching? Are you studying hard?"

"I was until today," I grumbled.

Anazian threw back his head and laughed. "Very bitterly said. You would rather be attending to Yallick's boring old lessons than hiking in the fresh air?"

His humor was infectious, and I grinned sheepishly. "Well, maybe if it were Spring it wouldn't be so bad."

"You just might be right, at that."

"Well, in answer to your first question, I guess things are going all right. Yallick seems to be satisfied."

Anazian looked closely at me. "He does? That's unusual."

That pricked my pride. "What's so unusual about that?" I snapped. "I'm a good student, and I work hard."

He laughed again. "No, no. You misunderstand. My apologies. What I meant was that it's unusual for Yallick to let a student know what he thinks. Especially if it's positive. I should know."

"Why?"

"I apprenticed with him, too." I looked at Anazian in surprise. He caught the look and said, "And now it's my turn to bristle if I choose. Does that seem so unlikely?"

I ducked my head in my own apology. "No. It's just that I thought it had been a long time since he'd had an apprentice."

"And so it is. I believe I'm considerably older than you think. The same is even more true of Yallick."

"But he's *ancient*. He must be at least fifty."

Anazian laughed aloud yet again. This time I noticed several mages look our way in curiosity. I wanted to tell him to stop, but didn't think it would do any good. He'd probably just laugh at me more.

"My dear girl, *I* am almost fifty. Yallick is over eighty. And even that is not terribly old for a mage. Or have they not told you that long life is another part of the gift?"

Yallick was over eighty? I couldn't believe it. He didn't look much older than Papa.

"I was Yallick's last apprentice. He said he would never take another, as I'd been so much trouble." There was a long pause in which I expected him to laugh again, but he didn't. Instead, he went on in a low voice, more to himself than to me. "I was quite surprised to hear he'd actually taken another." He gave me a sidelong look.

Disconcerted with Anazian's strange shifts of mood and conversation, I allowed myself to drift away from him.

We walked until about an hour after nightfall. I'd long lost track of both Yallick and Anazian in the ever-growing group. I hadn't seen Traz for some time, either, although every once in awhile I heard his boyish laughter rise above the murmured conversations all around me.

In the short time I'd been at Yallick's, I had met only a few of the other mages, and they were mostly the ones who lived nearby. As a result, I knew very few of the people now surrounding me, nor did they know me. Most would smile and perhaps nod if our eyes met, but no one seemed interested in speaking to me. I walked along and let my mind drift.

My fifth birthday. Breakfast, the traditional time for children to open their family gifts. Eight-year-old Breyard squirms excitedly in his chair, almost as if it's his birthday instead of mine. Mama reprimands him several times for his misbehavior, but she never catches me making faces back at him. Finally, the meal ends. Papa hands me a large, brightly wrapped and beribboned gift. I shriek in delight when I open the box to find it filled with wooden animals of every kind, all skillfully carved by Papa himself. Except for the whale, Breyard points out with pride. Then he hands me his gift, a box about eight inches square and four high. The contents of the box seem to shift even as I hold it. Mama and Papa obviously don't know what's inside and watch in curiosity. Breyard stands close as I unwrap it, staring into my face. I tear off the wrapping and open the box, and out slithers a small green and yellow snake. It's so sweet and soft. I let it twine around my fingers. This is apparently not the reaction Breyard expected, and his face falls.

CRACK! The sharp, resounding noise startled me out of my reverie. A streak of orange lightning shot overhead. Another, and then another, all from different directions.

"Everyone down!" Yallick's voice roared over the cries of surprise.

I heard the sound of running footsteps and then was knocked to the ground by something very large.

✦

The final play is in motion now. Ah, how proud Wals, DragonLord of old, would be to know of the fruition of his plan. The assault on the mages has begun by now. Once we have disposed of them, it will be easy to overpower the king, obsessed as he is with throwing his self-indulgent temper tantrums over the loss of the red dragon. He is like the legendary shavelle-mouse, which would eat until it burst if so allowed. We have given Erno free rein, and he engorges himself.

But I digress. My son has done his duty and will be richly rewarded. To shake his hand, to clasp him to my breast, to look upon his face. All the long years of sacrifice are worth what we shall gain, but I look forward to being able to speak with him again, father to son, son to father.

Has he married? Have I grandchildren hitherto unknown? Our final victory will bring the answers to these and so many more questions. It will not be long now—by Spring, I predict. The mages certainly cannot hold out against us longer than that.

Six

"Are you all right, Donavah?" Anazian's voice whispered right next to my ear as he pushed himself off me and rolled aside. I couldn't answer since he'd knocked the wind out of me. He placed an arm protectively over my shoulders. "I'm really sorry. I didn't mean to knock you down like that. I guess I misjudged in the dark."

I didn't say anything but just continued to lie there face-down, trying to get air into my lungs again and waiting to see what would happen. No more of the weird lightning bolts, but no one seemed inclined to rise until Yallick said it was all right. Next thing I knew, he was standing beside me, then crouching down, a hand on the middle of my back.

"Are you all right, Donavah?" By now I'd regained my breath, and I would have laughed at the way he asked me the exact same question Anazian just had, except that I was much too scared. The vibrations in the air all around exacerbated my fear, and the deep tension I sensed through Yallick's touch made it even worse.

"Yes, yes. I'm fine," I managed to whisper, my voice a little shaky. I pushed myself up onto an elbow and looked toward Yallick. "Anazian here was looking out for me." There was enough light from the moon for me to see the glint in Yallick's eyes as his gaze flicked to the other mage, then back to me.

"Stay here. Do not move until I return for you." Then he raised his voice just a little, and even though he was still whispering, he somehow projected his voice to everyone. "Remain as you are. I will investigate."

There were brief murmurs of conversation here and there, but Anazian didn't say anything to me. The minutes seemed to stretch into hours. I was sure it must be almost dawn before Yallick came back. And when he did, it was as if he appeared from thin air between eye blinks.

"All around is clear," Yallick announced in that same soft voice that carried to everyone. "We must move on quickly now."

He reached down a hand to help me to my feet. I'd grown stiff and cold sitting on the ground, and I was grateful for his assistance this time. "Stay by my side, Donavah," he said, taking my hand and leading me to the front of the group before letting go. I sensed that the responsibility for almost two hundred people weighed heavily on him, so I stayed near him despite a strong wish to find Traz.

Yallick didn't speak as everyone got underway again. I walked at his side, trying hard not to yawn and not succeeding very well. Then, after we'd been moving somewhat less than an hour, I heard Xyla's voice inside my head.

"Donavah? Something is wrong."

"What?" I asked her as my heart started racing again.

"Not with me. With you. What has happened?"

I explained quickly about the lightning bolts, then asked how far away from her we were.

"Not far. Close enough for you to hear me and me to hear you."

"Thanks for that, Xyla. I hadn't noticed." And I grinned.

Indeed, it wasn't long before we arrived at the rendezvous point to find the red dragon waiting patiently. She lay curled up, as usual, but I could see her eyes watching us. I ran to her and spread out my arms along her shoulder—the nearest I'd ever get to embracing her.

A lump rose in my throat when I thought back to the day, scarcely three months ago for me but who knew how long for her, when I held her, newly hatched on my lap. Neither of us had known then what our futures held together. But later she'd gone away, to Stychs, to mature and grow so that she'd be big enough to help me try to save my brother. A new thought struck me, and I leaned away from Xyla's shoulder and looked first at her belly and then at her head. Stychs must be where she'd gotten pregnant. Why hadn't I realized before?

I heard her chuckle inside my head.

"You sly lizard, you!" I slapped her affectionately.

Leaves rustled behind me and I turned to see Yallick approaching. Behind him, there was a flurry of activity as the mages set up camp for the night. I looked up at the stars and saw that it wasn't nearly as late as I'd thought.

"Xyla, my dear," Yallick said aloud, and that surprised me; why did he want me to hear what he said to her? "How do you fare?"

"Well," she said. "And you?" It took a moment for that to sink in. I was hearing her speak to Yallick. That had never happened before.

"It has been a tiring day," the mage continued aloud. "And more to come." His glance fell on me. "Donavah has told you what happened?"

"Strange lightning." And she actually shuddered.

"Yes. I do not know for certain what it means, but I fear . . . the worst. You must fly far ahead tonight. Not just a day's walk for a human. You must go to the mountains immediately. Tonight if you can get that far. Then send a bird back with word where we can find you."

I opened my mouth to object, but Yallick raised a hand to silence me.

"I understand," Xyla said, and there was fear in her tone. What could frighten a dragon?

We stepped back several paces as Xyla rose and stretched her wings. She leaned her head down over me, and I felt her breath stir my short-cropped hair.

"Be safe, child mage," she said. And with a great leap, she was gone. I wondered whether Yallick had heard what she said to me. He didn't speak as he turned back to the clearing where a number of fires crackled merrily. I followed him, almost in a daze.

At a fire a little apart from the others, Traz sat tending some concoction. He might be only ten, but his days serving as a kitchen boy at Roylinn Academy had turned him into an excellent cook. Before long, our supper was ready, and we all three dug in. I wanted desperately to ask Yallick why he'd sent Xyla so far ahead and out of reach, but I sensed that for now, he wished me not to say any more about it.

We finished eating, and I started gathering up the dishes. When Traz and I had traveled together, we'd agreed that one would cook and the other would wash up, so it seemed natural to fall into that pattern now. Yallick offered to help and picked up half the dinner things while I stood there speechless. In the dark, I couldn't tell if the look he shot me was mocking or pleading, so I just shrugged and went in the direction Traz pointed.

When we arrived at the noisy stream, Yallick nodded as if satisfied about something. "I know that you do not understand my purpose in sending Xyla so far away."

I crouched down and set my load of dishes in the water at the edge of the stream. "Yes, that's right. I don't. But you have a reason." A statement, not a question.

"I do. And I will share it with you. But I must ask you not to speak of it to anyone, not even to Traz. Do I have your word?"

I nodded, then spoke my agreement. "I won't tell anyone." I could feel his eyes staring intently at me, as if he were trying to read my mind. Or my heart.

"I doubt I should tell even you. But if I do not, I know that it will worry you to obsession, and I do not need that kind of energy distracting me."

I felt myself blush and was glad it was dark so he couldn't see. Whatever else I might think, I had to admit that Yallick understood me. A lot of the time, anyway.

He glanced around and moved closer to me. "Let us make as much noise as we can washing the dishes," he said softly. "Listen carefully." That definitely piqued my curiosity, but also made my stomach turn in fear. "I am afraid that Xyla would be in grave danger if she stayed in this area. I believe that it is not the Royal Guard who are after us, but," his voice dropped to a whisper I had to strain to hear, "the dragonmasters."

I dropped the pot I'd been scrubbing with a loud splash. Dragonmasters! Just the thought of those black-robed magicians who could control dragons frightened me. They'd captured Xyla once before with their magic; they could do it again. Yallick reached into the icy water and retrieved the pot for me. A rush of questions crowded my mind, but all that came out was, "How?"

"That, indeed, is the question. And if I knew the answer, I would not be half as fearful as I am now. The mages have lived for centuries unhindered. Then, almost upon the heels of Xyla's arrival, we are betrayed. And on our very first day journeying, we come under attack. I do not know what is happening, and it is unsettling me as I have never been before in my long life."

A spoon I held in one hand began to clank rhythmically on the pot I held in the other, and I couldn't tell whether it was fear or cold that caused the shaking. Yallick took my hand in his. Somehow, despite washing dishes in cold water, his hand was warm, and the warmth spread to me, up my arm and further, making my hair feel almost as if it were standing out from my head.

"I have sent Xyla away to keep her safe. But we will not be able to join her until we have shaken the pursuit, and that will be difficult with such a large group, mages though we all be."

+ + +

If Yallick had meant to put me at ease, he failed. I tossed and turned all night, and while that was bad enough in one's own bed, it was infinitely worse when camping out on the ground in Winter.

In the morning, I yawned through breakfast and breaking camp. At first I walked with Traz, listening to him grumble about not seeing Xyla tonight. It was hard to resist telling him why Yallick had sent her on. How could it hurt to tell Traz? But I'd given my word, so all I said was, "Yallick must have his reasons."

Traz looked at me and rolled his eyes. "Yeah. He's grouchy and wants to make the rest of us that way."

I laughed but dropped the subject.

When the sun was well and truly up and everyone's mood seemed to have improved, Yallick called me to join him. I noticed how the nearby mages slowed down a bit, allowing the space to grow between Yallick and me in the lead and the rest of the group. Anazian was nearest, and he had to be at least twenty feet back.

"I do not know how long we will be on the move, and I do not want to neglect your studies any more than necessary. We cannot do much, but what we can do, we shall."

"Sounds good to me."

Yallick gave me a sharp look, as if in disapproval of my light tone, but he didn't remark on it. "How are you bearing up under all the tension in the air?"

"What tension in the air?" And then I caught my breath. I had always been extremely sensitive to the life vibrations all around me. But until Yallick mentioned it, I hadn't even noticed their absence the past few days.

He frowned. "Do you not feel it? Between this gaggle of mages and the forest itself, the cacophony is palpable."

"I . . . I don't understand. I don't feel anything. That's very strange."

For several moments, Yallick looked deep in thought. Then his eyebrows shot up. "Try this. I know you cannot close your eyes as we walk, so it might not work. But try anyway. Clear your thoughts."

Just like the meditation routine. I tried to allow the rhythm of my steps to substitute for blocking out sight. I'd learned back at Roylinn that rhythm could work that way, although I'd never tried it.

Yallick must have been able to tell when my mind had cleared. "Now focus. Feel what is around you. Life. Heart. Thought. Song. Feel the forest."

It was as if a brick wall crashed down inside my head. Yes, I could once again feel the vibrations around me. The heart-beat of the forest. The thought of the earth itself. The song of the wind. And more. The agony of defeat. Fear of the future, of the present. Terror for an end. An end to what? I staggered under the burden. The screaming earth rose up and slammed itself against me.

What have the dragonmasters to do with us? Why do they pursue us? And more to the point, how did they find us?

All the world is in upheaval now. A red dragon. A powerful new mage. Our ancient nemesis attacking. Portentous signs indeed, but to what do they point?

Is this the darkest hour before the dawn?

Seven

I didn't pass out. But my collision with the ground didn't stop the onslaught of vibrational activity. I clamped my hands over my ears to try to lessen the effects, but since it was a spiritual awareness, that didn't work.

Yallick knelt next to me, and the mages began to draw near.

"Stay back!" Yallick's arm shot up and I felt power emanate from him. To me, he said softly, "Focus again." But I couldn't. He placed a forefinger in the center of my forehead. "Focus on this spot." That was easier. "Clear your mind. Concentrate on the place where my skin touches yours." I took deep breaths, slowed the beating of my heart, and tried to ignore the noise inside my head. And suddenly, it was gone. I blinked in surprise and sat up.

In such close proximity, I could see in Yallick's eyes a deep concern, almost like a father's for a terribly sick child. "What did you do?" I asked.

His expression turned quizzical. "Do?"

"The noise . . . the vibrations . . . it all went away. It's gone."

He let out a long breath, stood up, and pulled me to my feet. Then he beckoned the watching mages, in front of whom I saw a very anxious Anazian, and we started moving forward again.

"Well," Yallick said, cocking he head slightly to one side, "that was an interesting experiment."

I scowled at him, and he burst out in laughter that rang through the forest. A sarcastic remark rose to my lips, but I managed—just barely—to suppress it.

"In truth, I cannot teach you what you already know. I can only teach you how it works and how to control it."

Not in a mood to solve conundrums, I just kept walking and didn't say anything.

"Today I thought to teach you how to block outside vibrations. I know how sensitive you are, and with the air around us so unstable with them, I knew you must be struggling. Only I find that you have been blocking already."

My annoyance quickly turned into interest. "Blocking vibrations? You can do that?"

"Yes, I can do that. Been able to for more years than your father has been alive." He grinned and raised his eyebrows. I couldn't help smiling back. I wasn't used to this side of Yallick's personality, joking and laughing and all. It took some getting used to. "You can, too, Donavah," he said more gently now. "You *have* been."

"But how?"

"How you have been blocking without realizing it, I have no idea. I will teach you the theory so that you can understand the practice. Then you will have the power to control the skill." His voice fell into its usual teaching tone. "As in all things, control is the key. Control is power. As it turns out, you can block. You must now learn how it *is* that you can block, and how to unblock. This ability to control a skill allows you to use that skill more effectively."

He paused, as he often did during lessons, to let me absorb that. Or perhaps he knew that all the activity in the woods around us, as well as that of all the mages following, would be distracting. "We will work more on this later. Once you master it, you will be ready to learn how to control the vibrations you generate."

And with that tantalizing announcement, he ended the day's lesson.

+ + +

So it went on for the next several days as we headed northeast. Sometimes, I heard snippets of grumbling conversation, which were always cut off when the speaker noticed me nearby. I wondered whether Yallick had told anyone other than me that we weren't yet heading directly to meet with Xyla.

At some point during each day, Yallick had a short lesson with me. It took only two days for me to learn how to block and unblock vibrations at will. Once I knew what I was doing, it was so easy that I created my own challenge. Perhaps I could learn how to pick out a single vibration.

I decided it would be easiest to experiment with Traz. At first, I didn't tell him what I was doing. I'd unblock for a few moments when he was near and again when he was off somewhere else, trying to discern the vibration that was uniquely his. When I thought I had the knack of it, I told him what I was trying to do and enlisted his aid.

After supper that evening, he hid somewhere in the nearby woods. I unblocked and searched for the trace of his signature. There, faint. I headed into the trees. It grew a little stronger. Off to the left. A little way farther. On the other side of that tree, right there.

"Ha! It worked!" I exclaimed.

"I bet you just followed me," he said as we headed back to camp.

"Did not."

"Hrumph," he snorted, but I could tell from his vibration that he was only teasing. I also felt a small twinge of jealousy from him. If only there were something I could do to help.

Then, just as we reached the perimeter of the camp, a searing green flash filled the sky. Blinded by the light, I reached out for Traz, but my searching hand didn't find him. A deathly silence fell on the camp. Where others, less disciplined, might have burst into screams, the mages all stilled themselves. I unblocked to try to get a sense of what was happening, but while all might be still, the air was filled with pandemonium. I couldn't risk losing control of myself now, so I quickly blocked.

By this time, I could see again. The campfires blazed away in the night, but all around, the shadowy shapes of the mages rose to their feet. I tried to see where Yallick was, but couldn't.

Then green lightning arced across the sky and into the midst of the camp. Someone screamed, and I smelled burning flesh. Another flash of lightning and another scream. Sounds of panic and figures racing everywhere. Where was

Yallick? What should I do? I looked at Traz, but he wasn't next to me. I spun full circle to see where he'd gone, but I couldn't find him anywhere.

"We are discovered!" Yallick's voice boomed over all the other sounds. "Scatter!" As if everyone wasn't already doing that. Everything went dark as somehow, all the fires were extinguished. Lightning fell faster and faster now. I called out Traz's name, then Yallick's, but I couldn't even hear my own voice.

A sizzling sound split the air, and a bolt of the green lightning struck a tree only a few feet from me. Until now, I'd stood rooted in place watching the scene unfold, but the shock of the strike shook the ground beneath me and I fell down. That was enough for me. I scrambled to my feet and ran headlong in the opposite direction from the camp.

As I raced away from the confusion, lightning continued to strike all around. The forest animals were now trying as frantically as I was to get away. Birds that would normally be sleeping at night flew dazedly through the trees. Predators ignored their usual prey as both ran in the same direction.

There was shouting, some nearby, some farther off. Once or twice, I even thought I heard my name, but I didn't slow down to find out. All I wanted was to escape, and in double-time. I didn't know in what direction I ran, and I didn't care.

A loud thrashing noise came from my left, and whatever it was, it was moving a lot faster than I. It couldn't be a squirrel or a fox, not making that kind of noise. A wolf, perhaps? The fleeting thought that I had no way to protect myself was followed immediately by the creature itself. I took one glance and suddenly wished it were only a wolf. A huge wild boar tore through the undergrowth, heading straight at me.

I screamed. In the flashing green light, which was all behind me now, I caught a glimpse of a nearby tree with branches low enough to climb. If only I could reach it in time. I thought I'd been running at full speed, but now found I could sprint just a little faster. The heavy breathing of the creature was on my heels; I fancied I could feel its breath on my neck. Loud grunting noises and the thunderous pounding of its heavy feet . . . I wasn't going to reach the tree in time. A tusk caught on my cloak. Then, just as I thought maybe I'd make it after all, I tripped on something and fell in a heap. Instinctively, I covered my head with my arms and curled up into a ball. Mama's face flashed into my mind, then Papa's, and Breyard's. I waited for the huge tusks to rip into my unprotected flesh. My muscles tensed in anticipation.

A thud, and everything went quiet. Almost afraid to see what new threat had arrived, I opened my eyes. The boar lay on its side next to me, a tusk still poking through the rip in my cloak. I felt a strong power emanating from nearby, even though I was still blocking. Then Anazian came striding toward me, a look of intense worry on his face.

I let out my breath in a loud sigh, trying to release some of the tension as well. I started to stand up.

"No," Anazian said, "stay there. Let me make sure you're all right."

"I am," I assured him. "It didn't get me."

The mage dropped to one knee beside me, placing a hand on my shoulder. His chest rose and fell as his breath recovered from the chase. Mine was returning to normal, too. I let out a strained giggle when I noticed that we were breathing in rhythm.

"I really am all right," I said, appreciative of Anazian's concern, even if it was unnecessary.

"I'm glad I happened to be fleeing in the same direction as you," he said with a wry smile.

I looked at the fallen boar. "Me, too. Is it dead? How'd you kill it?"

He shook his head. "Not dead. Definitely unconscious, and if my spell was strong enough, it should stay that way for the rest of the night. But I had to prepare the spell hastily, so we should move away from here quickly, just in case."

We got to our feet, and continuing in the direction I'd been going, we fled.

✦

Move and countermove. We have them on the run. This has been the game of the ages, masterfully planned and exquisitely executed.

They don't yet seem to realize that they are nothing more than cat's prey now. And we can afford the time to toy with them. Some of the pleasure, indeed, will be in the chase. By the time they grasp the truth, it will be too late.

I wonder: will my glass show me the face of the last one as he dies?

EiGHT

We went on all night. Once Anazian determined we were far enough away from the boar, should it wake, we took a short break. I had nothing but my cloak, and I knew that before long, I would miss my things, especially my waterskin. But Anazian had his pack, and when we stopped for a short rest, he shared his water with me. Once we moved on, he refilled the skin at the first stream we came to.

The shock of the attack on the camp began to lessen a little, and I started asking Anazian questions.

"What happened? What was all that green lightning? And why . . . ?"

"Whoa! One question at a time! We have all night and then some. To begin with your second question, it was an attack by the Royal Guard."

I almost contradicted him, but remembered in time that Yallick had told me his fears about the dragonmasters in confidence. He obviously hadn't shared them with Anazian. It occurred to me that I might get more information if I pretended to know less about events than I really did. "How did the Royal Guard make the lightning? I thought they were strictly military."

"I thought so, too. Perhaps they've started working with the court magicians." He laughed at this, but I didn't see what was so funny.

"But why are they coming after us? What difference does it make?"

"If the king says to do something, the Royal Guard does it, no questions asked. My best guess is that it has to do with the dragon. The king hasn't been able to see reason on that topic ever since the egg was stolen. The rather, ah, dramatic show that you and Traz put on rescuing your brother didn't exactly improve the king's temper."

His way of putting it amused me. I supposed it had been "dramatic" at that, with Traz's staff emitting red lightning that broke the dragonmasters' net of spells and let Xyla get free.

"Anyway," Anazian went on, "I suppose losing the valuable rare dragon was just the excuse he needed to finally root the mages out of Alloway for good."

Something still didn't make sense. "But how did they find us so fast? The mages have been in hiding forever. If it was that easy, why didn't they do it before?"

"I don't know. If we knew the answer to that, we wouldn't be in this predicament now, would we?"

We walked on and on through the night, sometimes chatting about inconsequentials and sometimes in silence. I wondered if we might meet up with some of the other mages, if any had come this same direction . . . and hadn't turned back. I never once questioned why we were continuing; the thought of possibly encountering any of the Royal Guard terrified me.

Just before dawn, Anazian found a hiding place between several large boulders. He built a small fire. It felt good to warm my numb fingers and toes, and I was astonished to see absolutely no smoke. Anazian just gave me a mysterious smirk when I asked how he did that. He didn't answer the question, but instead suggested that I get some sleep while I could.

I pulled my cloak tight across my chest and lay down facing the fire. I wished for a blanket, but that didn't make me feel any warmer. For a little while, I gazed into the flickering flames, remembering the nights I'd spent traveling with Traz. Where was he now? Was he all right? I hoped he hadn't gotten separated from Yallick as I had. Well, at least I was safe with someone who'd been Yallick's apprentice. He must be a powerful mage in his own right. And with that, I fell asleep.

+ + +

I awoke feeling toasty warm and found that Anazian had covered me with his own cloak. He sat nearby wearing just his heavy wool trousers and tunic.

"Aren't you freezing?" I asked, sitting up.

"I wouldn't have shared my cloak if I were. Here." He grinned and handed me a tin cup full of steaming tea.

"Thanks," I said, curling my hands around it and taking a sip. "But how can you be warm enough. It's so cold."

"You will learn, my dear. All in good time. Did you sleep well?"

"Yes, thanks to you." I indicated the cloak. "Did you?"

He shook his head. "I didn't sleep. One of us needed to keep watch, and you were far too tired. It's a good thing I did, too. A small contingent of soldiers passed by a few hours ago." My heart leapt in fear. He must have seen it in my face. "Not to worry. It was no difficult thing to hide the fire from dolts like that." He handed me a piece of flatbread. "You better eat this so we can move on. With good luck, we will find the others today."

But we didn't have any of that luck. We travelled the whole day without signs of anyone at all. I noticed that we were heading northwest. But although I felt sure that we should be trying to turn more eastward, I didn't feel comfortable saying anything. Perhaps Anazian knew a circuitous route to the mountains.

As we walked that day, Anazian taught me all kinds of herb lore. I paid careful attention in hope of retaining as much of the knowledge as I could.

"See that winter-flowering herb there?" He pointed at a low, spreading plant with tiny pink flowers. "Thomwort, excellent for stomachache. You crush the flowers into a paste, mix in just the right amount of goat's milk, and administer two spoonfuls every four hours." He wouldn't tell me exactly what the "right amount" was, of course.

A little later, we came across a tall shrub with sharp thorns and green berries. "Winthistle, an effective cure for . . ." a pause as he gave me a mischievous look ". . . female troubles." I turned my head away a little in embarrassment, then hoped he hadn't noticed.

"Also good for strengthening nursing mothers."

We walked on. Since I'd slept until two hours after dawn, we didn't stop for lunch. In the middle of the afternoon, we took a short rest and ate some dried fruit. The all-night walk followed by only a few hours of sleep was beginning to tell on me, and I wondered how Anazian, who hadn't slept at all, could keep going. When he told me he wanted to push through as much of the night as possible, I wanted to snap at him that I was already tired, but I managed to hold my tongue.

Most of that night was a blur, other than something that happened around midnight. We'd discovered a path that led more or less in the direction Anazian wanted to go. I was in a fog of weariness, concentrating on just putting one foot in front of the other.

Anazian grabbed my arm and we both halted. His grip communicated his tension, even through all my heavy winter garb. He put a forefinger to his lips to quell any questions and, taking my hand in his, led me off the path and into the darkness of the woods.

It had been cold walking; standing still was even worse. It seemed as if hours had passed, and I was just about to ask why we'd stopped at all, when I heard clomping feet, jingling gear, and quiet voices. A troop of soldiers went past on the road. I held my breath and willed my heart to stop banging so loudly in my chest.

Anazian wore a look of deep concentration. His lips even moved a little. I'd have to ask him what kind of spell he was casting. Later.

Once the troop had gone by, I breathed a little easier, but I no longer had any inclination to move on, not for a long time. Anazian beckoned me to follow him much sooner than I would have liked.

I decided that it was long past time for me to stop blocking vibrations. That had probably been what tipped Anazian off that the enemy was so near. It had just been so easy to block that it hadn't occurred to me that I was cutting myself off from an important source of information.

When I first unblocked, the life vibration of the forest felt comfortingly familiar. Then I detected a subtle undertow of negative energy. I glanced at Anazian to see if he felt it, too, but he continued to stroll along as if nothing were wrong. It must be the residue from the soldiers who were now ahead of us.

Before long, the rush of energy that had accompanied the fear of discovery wore off, leaving me even more tired than I'd been before. Soon I was stumbling along, and finally Anazian realized that I couldn't go on any farther.

I was scarcely aware of him looking for a likely spot, building a fire, and telling me I'd be more comfortable sleeping on the ground than on my feet.

But I didn't sleep well. Dreams of flashing light, screams of pain, and the rattling of armor disturbed my slumber. I awoke several times, always to find Anazian staring into the flames. I had a nagging feeling that I should have offered to keep watch and let him get some rest, but I always fell back to sleep before I could form the words to speak them.

It turned out that Anazian wasn't able to hold out. When I woke up, well into the morning judging by the angle of the sun, I found him sound asleep and the fire burned down to embers. I rose as quietly as possible and rebuilt the fire with wood Anazian had gathered while I slept. Then I took the waterskin that lay empty next to Anazian's pack and went in search of water. The brook I found ran swift and cold. I splashed water on my face to wash away the last traces of sleep.

When I returned to the fire, Anazian was just sitting up and rubbing the sleep out of his eyes. He started when he saw that I was no longer lying in the place I'd spent the night, and I could feel his relief when he spotted me standing nearby.

"I can't believe I fell asleep," he said in an annoyed tone as he held his hands out to the fire.

"You obviously needed it," I said, setting the waterskin down. "It's been days since you last slept."

"That's no excuse. We could have been found, captured . . . or worse."

I almost asked what could possibly be worse than being captured by the Royal Guard, but decided I didn't actually want to know.

The day went much like the previous one, except that it was noticeably colder. This seemed to please Anazian. I wondered if it might make it harder for someone to track us, but I couldn't figure out how the temperature could affect that. If it rained, sure. But the sky was a clear, wintry blue.

I felt better for the rest I'd goten, but Anazian seemed irritable, as if falling asleep bothered him more than he was willing to say. He didn't talk as much as he had the day before, and as the afternoon progressed, the silence between us built until it felt like an impenetrable wall.

Finally, the sun went down, and Anazian surprised me by saying we'd stop for the night, that he knew of a good place just ahead. We walked about another half mile, then turned off the road onto a faint track that I wouldn't have noticed if he hadn't pointed it out. We followed the path a short way to a place where the trees grew thicker. He stopped at a point where they grew almost unnaturally close together.

Anazian nodded in satisfaction, and we set about making camp for the night. I started the fire while he went for water, then I cooked up a simple vegetable stew and he gathered more firewood.

After we finished eating, I still didn't feel quite sleepy enough to lie down. As we sat keeping warm in front of the fire, Anazian began to talk about the trees.

"This forest we've been traveling through—have you any idea of its age?"

I shook my head. "I never really thought about it. I guess it's been here forever."

He smiled. "Almost, perhaps, but not quite. The trees, they can tell you."

My eyes widened. "You can talk to the trees?" Maybe that explained why he was so knowledgeable about plants and so adept at finding his way through the woods.

"Oh, yes. Anyone maejic can. You need only to learn how. Would you like to try?"

"Yes!" I said eagerly. "I'd love that."

He rose to his feet and held out a hand to assist me. I took it with a smile. Maybe I could get used to this kind of gallantry after all.

He glanced around. "There. That one will do." I followed him to the one he'd chosen. A beech tree, with a pine growing right next to it, not two yards away. He placed his hands on the trunk of the beech and listened with eyes half closed.

A smile came to his lips. "Yes. Here. Place your hand on the trunk, like so."

Facing him, I stepped closer, putting my right hand where he indicated.

His voice softened. "Close your eyes. Feel the skin of the tree under your hand. Feel its sap flow in rhythm with your own blood."

I tried to do as he said, but I didn't feel anything but rough bark. Maybe this was something I'd have to work at harder than usual. I concentrated, but still nothing.

Anazian placed a hand on top of mine. It felt very warm, and I remembered how Yallick's had done the same all those days ago. I squeezed my eyes tighter in concentration, but it didn't help.

All of a sudden, I felt a crushing pain in my hand, as if the bones had been smashed to powder and the flesh pressed flat. My eyes flew open as I cried aloud. I looked to find my hand buried up to my wrist in the tree itself.

"What?" I gasped. "What's happening?" My voice rose to a panicked shriek. "Help me!"

Anazian struck me so hard across the mouth that my head snapped back. "Be silent, you fool!" I felt blood from a split lip trickle down my chin as Anazian reached for my other hand. I struggled against him, but it was useless. He captured my free hand and pressed it into the trunk of the nearby pine.

The agony doubled, and I couldn't help it: I screamed. But no sound came out of my mouth.

✦

The attack was brutal and effective. Klemma is gone. So, too, are Marby, Pellin, Forb, and Illid. Others are injured, and several of them may yet die. And still others—many others—are missing. Stam, Anazian, Doolh, to name only a few. And worst of all, Donavah.

The few birds I was able to summon after the attack sought out any trace of her vibrational signature. All returned having found nothing.

We must go on to Xyla, those of us who have regrouped. But for my apprentice, I must hold out hope against hope whilst I dread the worst. If she is lost, how very, very much more will be lost as well.

Nine

For a few moments, the pain threatened to engulf me. I took in great heaving breaths and tried to force myself to calm down.

Anazian's laughter rang through the woods. I blinked the tears out of my eyes and looked at him. He stood there scrutinizing me, hatred pouring from his very being. What had I ever done to him? Why was he doing this? I bit back the questions, not wanting to give him any more satisfaction than he was already getting.

"And that should settle you," he said, spitting out the words. "Pleasant dreams, my dear."

I could only watch in horror as he gathered his things, kicked out the fire, and strode off into the darkness.

I stood there; what else could I do? The chill soon began to seep into my joints, and I began to shiver. After awhile, I realized that the trees, too, shuddered periodically, as if the invasion caused them pain.

Attached to them inextricably, I tried to use my maejic to communicate with them. To no avail. It was some time before it occurred to me that despite having unblocked, I felt nothing. No vibrations of any sort.

New panic rose up inside me, and I had to work harder than ever to gain control. The feeling eventually subsided, but was quickly replaced with despair. Tears of fear and frustration welled in my eyes and spilled down my cheeks. I sobbed.

And discovered that I truly had no voice. I tried to speak. Nothing. I tried to hum. Still nothing. I tried every way I could think of to make noise, but not a sound escaped my lips. Anazian had made me mute, too. Unable to cry out for help. And what else might he have done?

The minutes crawled by. I soon became completely numb with cold. At least I could no longer feel the excruciating pain in my hands. I couldn't feel much of anything at all. Eventually, my thoughts themselves seemed to go numb.

The night passed with the agonizing slowness of a painful death.

Then, just after dawn, I heard a gasp behind me. I tried to look around, but I couldn't see anyone. All I could think of was that Anazian had returned for some horrible purpose, perhaps to gloat and watch me die.

"Is this what you meant?" a soft, deep voice asked. "I can see why you were so upset." I tried harder to see who was approaching, and I felt the muscles in my arms pull. "Stop struggling, before you hurt yourself." And the owner of the voice stepped into view and stood a few feet in front of me. It was definitely not Anazian.

A young man, probably in his early twenties. He wore buckskin leggings and tunic, and soft boots that let him walk silently when he wished. A mass of wavy black hair fell past his shoulders. Several knives of various lengths hung sheathed from his belt, and he leaned a long bow against the beech tree. But it was his grey eyes that drew and held my attention. Somehow, they conveyed a wealth of concern with a simple gaze.

He raised a hand slowly, as if he were trying to calm a frightened animal. "You'll be all right now." His voice was gentle. He took a step or two nearer, and I flinched. If I could have, I would have backed away. But trapped like a fly in a spider's web, I was completely helpless. At his mercy. Whoever he was, he could do anything to me. Absolutely anything.

He looked deep into my eyes. "It's all right. It really is." My breath eased the tiniest bit. "I'm going to help you. Look." He raised his other hand, so that I could see them both. He came a few steps closer. His eyes made me want to trust him, but I was simply too afraid.

He came yet closer, and he was now too near for me to maintain eye contact. He placed his hands on the trees, over my hands buried deep inside. I could feel his warm breath on my forehead. We stood that way for several moments, and then I felt my hands slip free. I collapsed in shock, and the young man barely caught me before I fell.

He carried me away from where I'd been imprisoned and set me on the ground next to the long-dead fire. I cradled my hands in my lap and bent forward, almost in a fetal position, while he hastily started a fire.

Soon its warmth began to thaw out my seemingly frozen flesh. But with the return of feeling to my limbs came also the return of pain to my hands.

I heard a snuffling sound, and before I could look up to see what it was, a cold, wet nose poked through my hair and touched my cheek. I sat up in surprise to find a white and brown hound looking at me, ears perked in curiosity.

"Leave her alone, Chase. Come with me now."

The hound looked at its master and back at me a few times, then sat down next to me, actually leaning against my thigh.

"Have it your way, then. By the way, I'm Grey. I mean, that's my name."

I opened my mouth to speak, but nothing came out. I looked away, embarrassed.

"I'm just going to get more wood. You stay here and get warm."

As if I could move anywhere. He left, and I felt panic begin to return at being left alone. The dog rubbed its head along my arm, as if it understood and was trying to reassure me. I raised a hand to pet it.

And found that both hands had balled themselves into tight fists. Nothing I could do would budge a single finger. I held my hands out to the fire, hoping that the warmth would loosen the joints. If anything, it just increased the pain.

When Grey returned, he found me rubbing my fists together furiously. He dropped the load of wood he was carrying next to the fire and knelt down beside me, taking my hands in his. He examined them one at a time and tried to prise thumb away from forefinger. His touch was gentle, but my hands might have been made of stone for all the good it did.

He shook his head. "That's bad. I don't know if I have the skill for this," he said in a worried voice. "Why don't you lie down now and sleep? I'll tend the fire and try to find something to eat." He stood up and walked away again.

At first, I felt reluctant to sleep, even though I was tired beyond belief. I tried to "speak" to Chase, but the dog didn't respond. My maejic must truly be gone. Still, Chase was watching me closely, and something about his manner reassured me about his master. I lay down and fell asleep almost immediately.

I awoke to the smell of cooking meat. I knew I should feel hungry, but instead the odor made me sick to my stomach. I didn't have the strength to stand; I just rolled over and crawled a few paces away before I vomited. Not much came up, but I felt a little better once it was gone. Then I crept back to the fire. Grey looked at me and then at the rabbit he was roasting on a stick.

"I don't know if you'll be able to keep this down," he said, "but you'll have to try. I went out this morning to hunt, not camp, so I can't do more than this. Unless you have food stashed somewhere?" I shook my head. "Well, we'll see how it goes. I want to try to get you to my house before nightfall. We'll need to leave soon." He took a knife from a sheath at his hip and cut into the rabbit. He sliced off a small piece and handed it to me. I reached out for it before I remembered about my hands. He frowned as he looked at my fist, then he looked at the meat, then at me. With a small, apologetic shrug, he held the meat to my mouth. I blushed, but there was nothing to be done but to accept his offer.

I ate what I could, which wasn't much, then Grey doused the fire. He helped me to my feet, and I took a few halting steps. How far was it to Grey's house, and could I actually make it there?

I stumbled along as best I could, but I never would have made it under my own power. Most of the way, I leaned heavily on Grey for support, and in the end, he had to carry me the last bit.

I scarcely noticed when he set me on a low pallet and covered me with furs. My last conscious thought was that it was nice to be so comfortable and warm before I died.

On the cusp of a new dawn, I can't help but think of those who turned away from us. Fools! True, most didn't survive a month beyond leaving us. How deluded they were to think they could simply turn their backs on us with impunity.

But there were those who had sufficient power to hide themselves. So sure in their self-righteousness that we would be defeated in the end. How they will tremble when they learn of their error.

And as our power waxes stronger than ever, we shall root them out. Traitors! They will certainly die a most painful and lingering death. And I shall relish watching.

ten

I don't know how long I was unconscious. I don't even know how long I was semiconscious—two or three days at least. Sometimes I was half-aware of things around me: a fire crackling on the hearth near where I lay; my hands swathed in aromatic poultices; Grey spooning broth, juice, or even wine down my throat; wind and rain howling outside; Grey taking care of things about my person that would have mortified me had I been fully awake; Chase curled up near me and sometimes even on the pallet as if he were keeping watch.

When I finally came fully to my senses, I wondered if it were all a dream. But, no. Although I was warm and comfortable, lying under several furs, I was in a place I didn't recognize.

The walls were of rough-hewn stone, and the ceiling had huge, dark-colored wooden beams. A fire snapped nearby. But when I pulled my hands from under the covers, they were still balled into fists. Useless lumps of flesh at the ends of my arms.

Chase let out a small whine, and a throat cleared.

"Awake now, are you?" And the man named Grey came over to me, a look of concern—maybe even worry—on his face.

I tried to speak, but my voice was still gone. The look on Grey's face was unbearable, and I turned away from him, rolling onto my side and facing the wall.

I wept. Tears poured from my eyes, and I couldn't even wipe them away. Silent sobs wracked my body, and my muscles tightened and cramped. And still I wept, until my stomach clenched and threatened to make me vomit. The nasty taste of bile in my mouth made everything worse.

When, finally, I regained some semblance of control over myself, I lay on my back again. Chase set his chin on the bed next to my face, and his breath warmed my damp cheeks. I reached up a hand to stroke him, but the sight of my fist threatened to send me back into tears. I let out a shuddering sigh and closed my eyes. Just concentrate on your heart, I told myself. Slow down its racing beat. Calm your breathing with deep, slow breaths.

Then Grey was there again, holding a steaming mug.

"Here," he said, his voice soft and deep, once again speaking as if to a trapped animal. Which, truly, I was. "Let me help you sit up and drink this."

When he slid an arm under my shoulders, my muscles tensed. All sense of calm fled, and I almost rolled away from him again. Chase whined, as if he were trying to speak to me. But I couldn't hear him. I should've been able to, but I couldn't.

Grey must have felt my passive resistance, but he didn't let it stop him. Instead, he lifted me up to a sitting position, then sat next to me, keeping one arm around my shoulders for support.

"Drink," he said, bringing the cup to my lips.

And I drank. I hated my helplessness but was too worn out from spent emotion to resist. This time.

The camomile tea laced with lavender loosened my tight chest. Breath seemed to come more easily. Chase wagged his tail and set his head on my knee. It felt awkward, but I rubbed a fist against the top of his skull. He closed his eyes in pleasure.

When I finished the tea, Grey helped me to my feet, and I took a few faltering steps to a chair placed near the fire. Grey sat in the other one, watching me intently. I wished he'd look away.

He finally broke the silence. "How are you?"

Once again I tried to say something—anything—-and failed.

Grey scowled in consternation. "I don't suppose this is some case of severe laryngitis?" I shook my head. "So you *can* actually talk?"

I nodded my head, then shook it, frustrated that I couldn't convey what I needed to.

"You can talk, but whoever did that to you back there," and he jerked a thumb over his shoulder, "did something that's taken your voice away?"

I nodded again, relieved that he'd understood.

"Hmm. Well, you seem to be feeling a little better."

I nodded yet again, wishing every kind of painful death possible on Anazian.

Grey stood up suddenly, startling me so that I cringed. He noticed and crouched down in front of my chair. His grey eyes bored into mine.

"Please don't be afraid. I'm not going to hurt you." His gaze held mine until tears filled my eyes again and I nodded. Though whether it was in agreement or just to make him stop looking at me, I wasn't sure.

He stood up in a slow, fluid movement and stepped to the hearth, where he stirred something that simmered in a pot hung over the fire. When he returned to his chair, he showed me a hand-carved mug and bowl.

"I made these for you while you've been ill. I left the bark on the lower part so it would be rough enough for you to handle yourself. I mean, with your hands like that." He looked away for a moment, almost as if he were embarrassed for his thoughtfulness. Well, considering what he'd done for me already, I was the one who felt embarrassed. I would just have to not think about it. "Anyway," he said, ignoring my blush, "I think I figured out a way for you to at least tell me your name. You're one up on me there, you know. I'll go through the alphabet, and you nod when I get to the right letter. Is the first letter a consonant?" I nodded. "B, C, D." Another nod. And so we went on until he'd gotten it all. "Donavah. Very pretty."

A silence grew between us that I could do absolutely nothing about. I wished I could get back into bed and sleep. Forever. Better yet would be to be home, where Mama could look after me instead of this stranger doing it. Where Papa could hold me in his arms and soothe my fears away.

"Well, you can't tell me much of your story, but I'm guessing you'd feel better knowing something about me."

He should've been right, but a sense of self-absorption had overtaken me. Now that my thoughts were beginning to clear, I found that I felt much more interested in thinking about myself, what had happened, and what would happen. I shrugged.

Grey took it as a sign to continue.

"You've probably already started wondering about my name. Well, from the moment I was born, my parents decided something was wrong with me. They gave me as little care as they possibly could. I guess my older sister pretty much raised me. Not that I remember very much of any of it. Just snatches here and there. My parents didn't even give me a name, just called me 'Grey' for the color of my eyes.

"When I was three, maybe four, they brought me way out here and left me with the hermit, Malk." A long pause, and bitterness hardened his eyes. "Or I should say left me *for* him. He wasn't home, so they tied a length of rope to my waist, tied the other end to a nail on the wall high out of my reach, and . . . and just walked away. Didn't even look back." Another pause during which Grey gave a violent stir to his cup of tea, causing some of it to spill over the side. I just watched, aghast at what he was telling me. "Malk didn't come home for three days, and I can only imagine his surprise at finding a half-dead toddler on his doorstep. He nursed me to health, and then raised me as the son he never had. Always called me Grey, since that was the only name I knew to tell him."

He looked searchingly at me, as if trying to decide whether he could trust me. Then he said, "Malk understood what was inside me. He didn't have the 'gift,' as he called it, himself, but he didn't begrudge anyone who did." I wondered what gift he could be talking about. Then he shook his head abruptly, as if to dispel his thoughts. "It doesn't matter. Malk was an accomplished magician and healer. He taught me as much as he could. And I was eager to learn it all. He died a few months ago, and now I expect that I will become the hermit-in-the-woods in his place."

He fell silent, and I wished more than ever that I could say something. Then Chase barked, causing us both to jump. Grey's hand reached reflexively for the knife at his hip before he realized that the dog was only barking at the pot on the fire. Grey laughed.

"So you think it's time for supper, do you, boy?" Chase wagged his tail, and if he could have, I'm sure he would have grinned. "Crazy dog. I sometimes think he should have been born human. He'd be better at it than some people I know." Grey arose and set about getting our meal ready.

The stew was delicious and rich with more healing herbs. The meat was so tender that it must have been simmering all day long. I felt sure that Grey had prepared it with care so that I would be able to slurp it without his help.

When the meal was done, I eased myself slowly to my feet. Grey watched me, poised in his seat to provide help if needed, but also apparently understanding my need for some bit of independence, no matter how small. I made it to the pallet and using both fists, managed to pull the furs over myself.

Grey moved to a pallet he'd placed near the fire. I watched drowsily as Chase lay next to him, curling up along his stomach. He scratched the dog's ears, almost as if it were an automatic reaction. Chase's tail thumped against the blankets in a lazy rhythm.

Grey began speaking. At first, I thought he was talking to Chase, but his voice was soft and the words felt into rhythm with the dog's tail. Then I realized he was telling a story, a bedtime story, something meant to ease me into sleep. I closed my eyes—indeed, I could scarcely have kept them open if I'd tried—and let Grey's soothing voice float into my thoughts.

"In the woods there once lived a wicked cobbler who liked nothing better than to make people miserable. He was magic, was this cobbler, and he used his power—meager though it was—to inflate his reputation until it was believed that he was the best cobbler in the land. People travelled from near and far to have shoes made by him.

"But the shoes never fit quite right. They were too tight or too loose. Perhaps one heel was slightly higher than the other. Or perhaps a few nails poked through the sole.

"Despite the discomfort, though, people still wore the shoes because they were, after all, the height of fashion.

"So much so that the king himself sent his daughter to the cobbler to have him make her wedding shoes."

But I never heard the end of the tale, for at this point, I fell fast asleep.

+ + +

I dreamt that night. I traveled by foot through woods in the dark, and as I walked, I realized someone was looking for me. It could only be Anazian! I blocked my thoughts, trying to merge myself with the darkness. "Donavah! Donavah!"

Voices cried from high over my head. Voices I recognized but couldn't place. I hid deeper and deeper inside myself, not wanting to allow any danger to get through my defenses. Then my ears filled with Anazian's laughter, and this time, he pressed my whole body into a huge oak tree. I screamed as life was crushed out of me.

I awoke bathed in sweat. I screamed again, this time for real, but, of course, there was no sound. A dog let out a yip, and a shadow rose from the floor and came over to me. I shrunk back against the wall, but the man kept coming toward me.

I pushed the covers away and practically launched myself from the bed. The man reached out, but I avoided his grasp and ran for the door. Outside would be safer than inside. Out there were places I could hide, not like in here. No one could hurt me if I could just get outside.

The complicated latch on the door defeated me. The man grabbed my shoulders and pulled me away from the door. With all the might that fear can pour into a weakened body, I struggled. I kicked. I struck out with my fists. My blows connected, and my adversary let out several grunts of pain. But in the end, naturally, he was stronger than I. He gathered me into his arms and held me tight against his chest, imprisoning my arms to that I couldn't hurt him.

In impotent rage, I sobbed. And the man stroked my hair.

"Donavah," he said. "Donavah. It was just a bad dream. You're safe with me."

And then I remembered Grey. It was he, not Anazian, who held me, who soothed me. It was Grey I was with.

The panic evaporated, leaving me weak and scarcely able to stand. Grey picked me up, with no more effort than if I were Chase, and carried me back to my bed.

"Let me make you some tea, something to relax you, help you get back to sleep," he said as he pulled the blankets and furs over me.

I shook my head. Shame overtook me, and I rolled over, once again turning my back on Grey. If only Papa were here. He would make everything better. I began to shake from a combination of emotion, weakness, and frustration. Grey placed a hand on my shoulder, as if to try to comfort me, but I shrugged it off. I didn't want him near me, didn't want him to see what I'd become.

After a few minutes, I heard him move away, presumably to lie down again on the pallet in front of the fire. I lay awake for a long time after that, afraid that I would slip back into my dream. Grey's breathing grew regular, and still I didn't sleep, not until dawn's light began to show in the window.

+ + +

When I finally awoke the next morning, the episode of the night before might have been all my own imagination for all that Grey said about it. His bruised jaw and split lip proved, though, that it had really happened.

He helped me to the chair again, tucked a fur around me to make sure I stayed warm, and filled my bowl with porridge, all without saying a word about what had happened in the night. But every time I caught sight of his face, I blushed and looked away.

When I finished eating, he gave me tea in which I could identify easing and healing herbs. He certainly knew his healing lore. Once I was settled, he began preparing his things to go out.

"I have to hunt," he said. "I still don't have enough stores set by for the Winter. But I won't go far, and I'll check back in on you when I can."

I nodded in acknowledgement.

While he was gone, there was little for me to do but sit and think. I did plenty of both. Why had Anazian turned traitor to the mages? Why had he tried to kill me? Why had all of this happened?

And what prospect for anything like a normal life did I have now? Virtually unable to communicate, would I simply molder away here, a parasite on a stranger until I finally died in some far-off future?

My thoughts started out dark and grew blacker over the course of the afternoon, although the two times Grey stopped in to check on me, I gave him a warm smile. No point in keeping him from what he needed to do.

Around dusk, I dozed off, only to be awakened by Grey stamping his feet on the doorstep outside and shouting for Chase to come inside. As soon as Grey opened the door, the dog came tearing over to me, wagging his tail and snuffling at me in obvious pleasure.

From the careful way Grey looked at me, I realized that he must've seen through the window that I'd fallen asleep and had made all that noise in an effort to keep from startling me awake.

Knowing this didn't improve my mood. I had an overwhelming sense that I was doomed to be nothing but trouble for the rest of my days.

Grey prepared our meal and hung the supper pot over the fire to cook, then settled into the other chair.

"Well, that was a good day's work," he said. "Another two or three like that and we'll be set for Winter." I wondered if that "we" included me, or just himself and Chase. I didn't know which would be my preference.

Chase sat in front of Grey, his head on his master's knees. Grey scratched his ears, making the dog groan in delight. But he watched me. I couldn't look him in the eye, but felt his gaze on me as I watched the flames under the pot.

"Chase turns four years old tomorrow," Grey said.

The irrelevance of this fact jarred my thoughts out of their rut. Grey grinned when I glanced over at him.

"When I was eighteen, Malk took me deep into the woods, four days' ride away. And left me on foot to find my way back." Remembering that his family had abandoned him, I could hardly believe that Malk had done this, and my shock must've shown on my face. Grey chuckled. "No, nothing like that. It was a test he'd prepared me for, one that I was anxious to take so that I could prove myself. I had all my hunting and traveling gear, just no food and a long way to walk. It wasn't easy, for the hunt sometimes took me in the wrong direction. But I got home—earlier than Malk expected and for which he was very proud.

"In anticipation of my success, he'd gotten me a pup from a litter borne to one of his cousin's bitches. When I got home, this little guy," and he gave Chase's head another scratch, "piddled himself, he was so happy to meet me."

Chase yelped, as if indignant at Grey's words. I couldn't help smiling—a real, honest smile.

"That's better," Grey said. "He was such a cute little creature, chasing bits of fluff blowing across the yard, and later mice and rabbits. I trained him myself, although hunting is in his nature and it wasn't exactly hard work. And he's been the perfect companion, especially since Malk died." He moved to the fire to check on supper and gave it a good stir before replacing the lid. "And now," he continued, his back still to me, "I have two companions." He turned to face me, and his face was serious, the expression in his eyes gentle. "Don't I?"

A lump rose in my throat. Grey didn't know the first thing about me, yet he cared. He cared about what happened, and he wanted to help me get well. I didn't understand how I could know these things, but they suddenly seemed obvious. I swallowed the lump and nodded, willing myself not to start crying again.

✦

Day and night, I send forth my thought seeking my apprentice. To no avail. I cannot find her. Xyla remains adamant that Donavah is alive, but even she cannot detect a trace of the girl.

We fly out several hours each day, but the dragon can do no more than that in her condition, and it is not enough.

Sometimes, as I sleep, I seem to feel the lightest touch of her consciousness, but when I awake, it is gone. I am sure it is nothing more than wishful thinking infecting my dreams.

Eleven

Over the next days, I grew stronger thanks to Grey's skill in healing. At first, it was awkward for both of us with me not being able to converse. Then Grey came up with something to help me communicate with him. He took a cloth about two feet square and, using a charcoal stick from the fireplace, wrote the alphabet on it, each letter large enough that I could easily point to it with my fist.

This meant I could now tell him things, like where I'd grown up, how I was feeling, and what I'd like to eat for supper, but it didn't lend itself to long conversations or explanations. I wasn't sure I wanted to tell him about Anazian anyway, and I couldn't tell him about losing my maejic.

I tried hard not to fall into black moods, but with no way to communicate meaningfully with Grey, and with nothing to do but think, sleep, and think some more, it seemed inevitable that my thoughts would slip into the same patterns: wanting to go home, wanting to be back with my friends, wanting anything other than what was actually happening.

Somehow, Grey always seemed to know just when my emotions felt as if they were going to explode, and he'd tell me a funny tale or joke to make me laugh. One especially rainy day, he managed to drag out the details of a particular story the whole day, building up disaster upon disaster until

I couldn't wait to discover what it was all about. When he finally reached the end of the story, where the man dies in a freak accident without ever getting to the bottom of it all, I laughed so hard I cried and my stomach muscles hurt.

Every night, after tucking me into bed as if he were my father, Grey sat on his pallet and told me another bedtime story. His soft, deep voice always lulled me to sleep before he reached the end.

But all his care couldn't stave off the unwelcome dreams. Dreams in which people hunted me. I could never see exactly who they were, for something always obscured my vision; I only knew that I didn't want to be found. Sometimes I thought I recognized voices: Papa, Yallick, Breyard, even Xyla. But I also knew that it could just as easily be Anazian, trying to deceive me so that he could have another go at killing me. I kept myself hidden.

+ + +

It hadn't come as a surprise to me that Grey meditated; after all, he'd been raised by a magician and I was sure he was magic himself. The first time I joined him, however, his eyebrows shot up, but he didn't say anything. I sat down several feet from him so as not to disturb his own energy field. I closed my eyes and tried to find my calm center, but it was as if Anazian had stolen that from me along with my voice and my maejic. Was even the magic gone? Still, going through the motions brought me some comfort and peace of mind, so I continued to join Grey for morning and afternoon meditations.

Sometimes, especially in the mornings when Grey was hunting, I would sit quietly, concentrating on making Chase hear me. I'd been surprised the first time Grey left and instructed the hound to stay with me. After all, the whole point of having a hunting dog was for it to help hunt. But I was glad of the company, and it gave me a chance to try to regain my maejic.

Not that it worked. And the frustration of not being able to speak or use my hands, being far from my family and friends, not to mention losing my power, overwhelmed me several times a day. One night, as I sat on the edge of the bed, I dropped my cup, spilling tea all over the floor. Grey looked up from repairing a tear in a leather garment just in time to see me stamping my foot. Embarrassed, I burst into tears. He came over and sat next to me. I wished he would go away and leave me alone. Instead, he put an arm around my shoulder and just sat there without saying a word. It reminded me so much of the way Papa used to comfort me when I was little—like when Breyard would tease me in front of his friends—that I sobbed even harder. Grey didn't say anything; he just held me and wiped my tears away.

As the days went by, Grey spent more time away each day, sometimes coming home well past midday and apologizing profusely for leaving me so long with nothing to eat. Once home, he spent some time outside in the lean-to shed behind the house. Something about his activity had an almost frantic edge to it, as if he were rushing to get everything done before full Winter hit.

But if he were making preparations for that, then that meant I was going to be stuck here—like this—all Winter. I couldn't bear the thought. To be a virtual invalid, cooped up alone for months with someone I scarcely knew? No, I had to get away, somehow find my way to the mountains and Xyla. That made me think of Yallick. Who didn't know of Anazian's treachery. For the first time, it occurred to me that I needed to find Yallick and the other mages. But how could I possibly tell Grey that I needed to find someone when I had no idea where they were?

Late that afternoon, I heard strange stamping and whistling sounds outside. I managed to pull a fur around myself and hold it clasped between my fists while using my elbows to throw the latch on the door. Walking outside was like stepping into a new world. The air knifed into my lungs, yet it was marvellously invigorating. Fresh air! Chase came around the corner of the house and raced over when he saw me, his tail wagging.

I followed the way he'd come, and when I turned the corner, my mouth dropped open at the sight that met my eyes. A large black horse with white stockings and a white blaze stood snorting and pawing the ground whilst Grey strew fallen leaves on the ground of the shed.

"I know it's not what you're used to, old boy, but it's only for one night."

Chase barked, startling Grey, who turned and saw me standing there.

"Oh," he said, looking a little embarrassed. "Well, um, I was going to tell you tonight, you see, and . . . Hey, you shouldn't be out here. Let's go back inside."

Chase let out a little whine while I gave Grey a look that meant, "You better explain yourself, and right now."

Grey looked at the hound and back at me, then shrugged. "Well, if we're going to beat the worst of the weather, we have to leave tomorrow."

I stood there in the icy air watching him finish bedding down the horse, whom he called Hallin, for the night. What did he mean, "leave"? Where were we going? From what he'd told me, it wasn't as if he had family with whom we could spend the Winter. What did he have in mind?

Grey gave Hallin a last swat on the rump, picked up a largish bundle, and closed the door of the shed. I followed him back inside. The warmth from the fire wrapped itself around me like one of the furs. Grey dumped his bundle on the kitchen table, then set about making tea, all the while maddeningly saying nothing.

When we'd settled in front of the hearth, Grey in a chair and me on the bearskin rug with the alphabet cloth next to me, both of us blowing on steaming mugs of herb tea, Grey finally spoke.

"I didn't say anything before because I wasn't sure I'd be able to get the horse, and I didn't want to get your hopes up."

I raised my eyebrows in question.

"Well, you know, to go find your people. Get you back to someone who can take care of you properly."

My jaw dropped. It was as if he'd read my mind. But how, I thought yet again with a frown, would I ever find Xyla and Yallick and everyone? And how many of them were left? Were any of them?

Grey misinterpreted my frown. "Donavah, we have to go, and we have to go now. It's already late enough in the season that we'll be lucky to get where we're going without any trouble from the weather."

I shook my head again. He set his mug on the ground, knelt in front of me, and gripped my upper arms in his strong hands. "We must. And we'll manage. Trust me."

He was right. And I wanted to go. The only problem was the significant fact that I didn't know *where* to go. Still, going would be better than staying. I smiled at Grey and nodded.

He sat back in his chair, breathing out a sigh of relief. That took the edge off my smile. Was he really that anxious of be rid of me? Well, if that were the case, all the more reason to get going.

"So, where?" he asked.

And with scarcely a twinge of guilt, I simply spelled out, "mountains."

"All right, east. I know the land well between here and the foothills. We'll start in the morning." We both sipped our tea simultaneously. The end of another almost completely one-sided conversation.

After supper, Grey suggested that I turn in early. The journey was going to be tiring for me, he said, even though I'd be riding Hallin. He wrapped my hands in poultices as usual, and I could smell a new ingredient that he'd not used before and that I couldn't identify. I wondered what it was, but before long, I fell asleep.

Grey awoke me well before dawn. While I ate a bowl of very sweet, very hot porridge and drank my tea, Grey went outside and nailed a heavy piece of lumber over the glass window.

Next to the door sat several full packs: a backpack for Grey and what must be saddlebags for Hallin.

The hammering stopped and a moment later, Grey came in.

"Are you just about ready?"

I smiled wryly as I nodded; after all, what exactly would keep me from being prepared to go at a moment's notice? I'd arrived empty-handed, and empty-handed I would leave.

Grey finished readying the house for our departure. He threw the furs from my sleeping pallet over the back of the chairs to let them air, then he washed the breakfast things and shoved my cup and bowl into one of the saddlebags. Finally, he dumped water onto the fire to make sure it was out. Then he wrapped me up in my cloak, another of his cloaks, and a fresh fur, which he secured around my shoulders with a metal clip. He stuck a floppy felt hat on his head and a bearskin one on mine.

A few minutes later, I found myself astride Hallin, with Grey fastening the packs to the saddle. The horse stamped impatiently while Grey nailed the door to the house shut. His nonchalant air suggested that he was accustomed to shutting up his house this securely. He hoisted his pack, and soon we were on our way.

Holding Hallin's reins, Grey started down a track that led roughly east away from his house. Chase ran off ahead, dashing back to us every few minutes as if to make sure we were still coming.

"You crazy dog," Grey called after him one time. "You know you only end up covering twice as much ground as I do this way." I laughed, silently of course. He looked up at me. "He's always like this, but once we start home with me riding Hallin, I'll really be able to wear him out."

I winced inwardly a little. At some point, I would have to admit to Grey that I didn't actually know where we were supposed to be going. And then I wondered whether Grey might like to stay with the mages—and me—when we found them. *If* we found them. But then, what reason might there be for him to want to? Surely he wanted to get back to his life, the one he'd had before I interrupted it.

All of a sudden, I wanted very much to be friends with Grey. Sure, I knew quite a bit about him, but he knew nothing about me, nothing important, anyway. I wanted us to be able to sit and talk, maybe watch a sunset or tell each other what we saw in the clouds. To sit up late over cup after cup of tea, speaking of the things that were most important to us. To introduce him to my family, my friends. Even if I shouldn't, I wanted to tell him about how I could use maejic—to dance a day away, to lift a boulder the size of a house, to create an image from a few stray strands of thought. Or had done once.

But maybe I'd never do any of those things again. Maybe Anazian had stripped me of everything it had meant to be me.

Chase, far ahead of us, started up a racket of barking that resounded through the forest around us, snapping me out of the morass of thought I'd fallen into. He came tearing up to us, his manner frantic. Grey stopped, and so did Hallin.

"What's wrong, boy?" Grey asked, taking Chase's head in his hands and looking searchingly into the hound's eyes. Something cold touched my neck, and a shiver went down my spine. Before I could figure out what it was, a few white flakes settled on Hallin's black neck. Grey laughed and rose to his feet. "You ridiculous animal! Behaving as if you've never seen snow before." Shaking his head, he took Hallin's reins, and we went on.

At first the snow was a pleasant diversion. As a child, I'd always loved the first winter snow. There was something enchanting about seeing the world obscured by a blanket of white. Not that it remained pristine for long with a brother like Breyard. When we were young, he'd rush out, before Mama could bundle him up properly, and begin to prepare for his assault. Ignoring Mama's shouts for him to come back, he'd scoop up great handfuls of snow and make snowball after snowball, stacking them neatly by the garden wall to be ready for the impending battle. Once I was big enough to make missiles of satisfactory size, he enlisted me to help him. It was his plan to win the first snowball fight. Village tradition, going back several generations, was that the first battle each Winter was a complete free-for-all. The top two combatants were duly assigned the title of "general," and they picked their armies from the rest of the boys. These armies spent the Winter battling for snow supremacy. Breyard had been general for the last three years before he'd left to study at Roylinn.

As my mind drifted, the snowfall grew heavier. Grey peered up into the sky to try to read the weather in the clouds.

"This is very strange," he said, coming to a stop. "There was no sign of a snowstorm coming or I wouldn't have left. Maybe we should go back."

I shook my head violently.

"Perhaps you're right. Maybe it'll stop soon. At least it's pretty. But it'll be cold camping tonight."

I hadn't thought of that, but the thought of turning back threatened to send waves of panic through me. We couldn't turn back now; we just couldn't. Every step closer to the mountains was one step closer to people who could help me.

We kept on through the day, not stopping for a midday meal. I wasn't hungry anyway, and Grey just ate as we went.

It kept snowing, and all afternoon we made our way through a fresh, wintery landscape. If we'd been out in the open, the snow would probably have been more than six inches deep. Since we were in the woods, it wasn't quite so bad, but it still slowed us down, especially Chase, who didn't venture far ahead all afternoon.

Despite the fact that I hadn't done anything all day except sit on a horse, I was exhausted by the time Grey halted for the night. The spot he'd chosen to camp was heavily wooded and protected from the prevailing wind by a huge boulder. He helped me off Grey's back, and as I walked around a bit, I discovered how stiff I'd gotten. I'd be sore—very sore—in the morning. Grey started a fire, and while he prepared supper, I did some stretches. He laughed when I winced in pain, and I shot him the dirtiest look I could, which only made him laugh more. I shook my head in mock disgust, imagining how I'd pay him back, if only I could. Say, a handful of snow down the back of his shirt.

And just then, a mass of snow dropped off a branch above and onto Grey's head. He shouted in surprise, jumped to his feet, and shook the stuff off. Chase barked in glee. I would have laughed had the coincidence been less uncanny.

Grey looked up just in time to get a faceful of snow. A groaning sound seemed to come from all around us, and I got to my feet, ready to move away from this new threat.

Suddenly Grey shot to my side and pulled me away from the fire, just as the trees shed their load of snow. With a huge *FLUMP*, the flames were out and our dinner buried. Chase barked even louder, but Grey just stared.

"Never seen anything like that happen before," he said, shaking his head. "But then, I don't usually build quite so big a fire. See what I get for trying to keep you warm?"

I looked at him in surprise, but found him looking side-long at me with a smirk. I clouted his shoulder with a fist, then motioned to the fire.

"Yes, ma'am. I'll get right on it." He quickly set about clearing the snow away and restarting the fire.

As supper cooked and Grey gathered more dry wood for the night, I thought about the day. Grey seemed to have relaxed, as if outside, he was in his element. Everything had felt awkward back in the house, almost formal, as if my presence made him feel like a visitor in his own home. Out here, he was joking around with me, and I was beginning for the first time to feel comfortable around him. All in one short day.

After we'd eaten, there didn't seem to be much point in trying to stay awake. It wasn't as if we could chat. I yawned.

Grey took several heavy blankets and an oilcloth out of a saddle bag. He lay everything out neatly, then patted the bedding.

"Time for beddy-bye."

I smiled and gave him a playful knock on the side of his head.

"You go to sleep, and don't worry about anything. I'll tend the fire."

He helped me bury myself in the covers, including the cloaks and my fur. I felt almost warm enough as I drifted off to sleep.

✦

Word has arrived from my son. All goes according to plan. The mages have been scattered and many killed. Fortunate ones, who went to their deaths unaware of impending defeat.

Today, for the humor of it, I tested Wals' Cursed Book of Secret Knowledge. I forced a lowly scribe's apprentice to try to read from it. No sooner did she set eyes to the page then she fell over in convulsions. Long she agonized. I wearied of her noise and had her carried away. They reported back that it was many hours before death came.

How many others have performed this test? How many have failed it?

Twelve

My body might have been stiff, sore, and in need of rest, but my mind churned through the night, leading me from one bad dream to another. I had that strange feeling of being aware that I was dreaming but not being able to wake up.

I ran through a pathless forest, zigging and zagging this way and that. It was a matter of great urgency, but I didn't know whether I ran toward something or away from it. The forest turned into clouds, and I was flying, soaring above the treetops, gliding effortlessly over mountains. Then I faltered. Down, down, I plummeted to the ground. It rose quickly, and there was nothing I could do to arrest my speed as faster and faster I fell. I landed facedown, but didn't die. My heartbeat sped up. Then I was being crushed; a heavy weight against my back pressed me into the gaping earth.

I awoke with a start in a terrified sweat. Weight pressed against my front and back. My heart thumped frantically in my chest and in my ears, and I could scarcely breathe. I gasped for air and pushed myself upright, tears streaming down my cheeks.

"What? Huh?" Grey's voice behind me. I swivelled around to find him lying under the covers next to me. He sat up in alarm. "What's happened? Donavah?"

Chase's cold nose touched my cheek, then he licked my chin a single time.

Aother bad dream, that's all it had been. I tried to gain control over myself, but failed. Grey drew close to me, wrapping his arms protectively around me. At first he seemed tentative and awkward, as if unsure how I would respond. But it was a surprising relief to let myself go. I wept harder than I yet had, quickly soaking the front of Grey's shirt with my tears. He just held me, sometimes gently stroking my hair or patting my back.

As my emotion spent itself and the fear subsided, I relaxed against his chest. I could hear his strong heartbeat, reassuringly slow and steady. When I finally grew calm, Grey took my chin in his hand and turned my face up to his. He looked deep into my eyes. I wished more than ever before that I could say something, then realized that I had no idea what I would say. But I didn't look away.

A log on the fire chose that moment to break apart with a small explosion, startling us all and making Chase let out a sharp yip.

"I better tend the fire." Grey let me go and rose to his feet. I watched him as he moved with catlike grace, every motion compact, every sense alert to what was going on around him. A true woodsman. With a heavy stick he knocked the pieces of burning wood together until they were a heap of red-hot coals, then he placed a large log atop the pile. "Um, I suppose I should have mentioned something, but you fell asleep before I could." I looked at him in confusion. "I mean, well, you know, sleeping with you. No, I mean . . ." His voice trailed off, and though it was too dark to see, I felt sure he was blushing. "I mean, if we share the blankets, we'll be warmer. So that's why I was sleeping with you like that—back to back. Chase must have curled up against your stomach. That's probably what woke you up."

Well, not quite, but I couldn't explain it to him, so I just nodded and smiled my understanding.

"Is that all right? I, um, I don't want to make you feel uncomfortable."

If he'd wanted to do something to harm me, he could have done it long ago without going to the trouble to bring me out here. I patted the bedding next to me, then lay down on my side and pulled the blankets over myself. Chase nosed his way under the covers and curled up along my stomach again.

For several more minutes, Grey crouched by the fire, poking the embers and adding another small log. Once he was satisfied, he came back to the improvised bed. He slid under the covers and lay down, his back to mine. Now the weight around me made me feel safe, and the last thing I heard before I dropped off into a contented sleep was the gentle popping of the campfire.

+ + +

I didn't wake up again until first light. Chase still lay next to me, curled up against my hip. Grey was heating water over the freshly stoked fire, but the spot where he'd lain next to me was still warm. I sighed silently as I sat up, rubbing my eyes with my fists.

Grey noticed the movement and looked at me with a shy smile. Nothing had happened; we'd only slept under the same blankets. But that had been enough to change our relationship.

Grey came over and helped me into my cloak. As long as I stayed near the fire, which he'd built high, I was warm enough. The snow had continued falling through the night, although the thick woods in which we'd camped had protected us from the worst of it. Still, it would make traveling today even slower than it had been yesterday.

Once we'd all eaten breakfast—Chase and Hallin, too—Grey broke camp. I helped kick snow and earth onto the fire, and soon we were on our way again.

For the next two days, our eastward progress was slow but steady. I began to get more and more nervous about having to admit to Grey that once we reached the mountains, I had no idea where to go.

On the fourth morning, we'd been underway for an hour or two when the wind kicked up and the temperature dropped. Chase drew close to Grey, who looked at the sky with a worried expression.

"This weather is very strange. It feels like a blizzard, but there weren't any signs that one was coming. If it gets worse, we're going to have to stop or else risk getting lost in the storm."

Soon, the snow was falling so heavily that we couldn't see more than a few feet ahead. Wind swirled around us in every direction, and Grey's hat went flying. Chase darted after it and brought it back.

We halted. Grey had to shout to make himself heard over the howling wind.

"We better build a fire now while we still can—if we still can." He helped me off Hallin's back. I stood leaning against the steaming shoulder of the horse while Grey gathered wood and started a fire next to a large boulder. I drew near and held out my hands, wishing the heat of the flames would finally loosen my fists and return the use of my hands. I was so tired of being useless and—worse—helpless.

Soon a large pile of wood lay ready near the fire. Grey took the bedding out of Hallin's packs, and we huddled up together, wrapping blankets around ourselves. Grey put a tentative arm around my shoulders, and I leaned against him. His chest rose and fell in a quick sigh. Despite the weather raging around us, I suddenly felt comfortable and cozy.

We sat, just listening to the wind roar. Every once in awhile, Grey tossed more wood onto the fire. Chase sat in front of us, his back to the fire, wagging his tail. I reached out and rubbed the top of his head with my knuckles.

The snow fell thicker and faster, piling up high beyond the reach of the fire's heat. And still we sat in companionable reverie.

Chase's whine startled me out of a doze. I tried to figure out what was unsettling him, but saw nothing except the fire, the wood pile, and deep drifts of snow. Grey looked around, too, and when he saw how high the snow had piled, he jumped to his feet, cursing.

Hallin stamped at Grey's abrupt movements. I immediately missed Grey's body heat and pulled the blankets more tightly around me. He walked around the circle trying to see over the top of the drifted snow. He shook his head.

"We might have a problem. I've never seen anything like this." He stopped on the far side of the fire, staring out across the snow. "It's . . . well, it's unnatural."

At those words, my heart seemed to skip a beat. Had Anazian discovered that I'd escaped his trap? If he had, could this storm be caused by him? Could he actually control the weather?

My heart raced and I began to panic at the thought of Anazian trying to find me, and while I couldn't do much, I *could* calm down.

I closed my eyes and concentrated on slowing my heart, my breathing, my thoughts. I sought my calm center, and to my surprise, found it. I held onto it like a lifeline. I still couldn't feel any life vibrations around me, but I tried to create my own rhythm.

I began rocking ever so slightly to the pulse of the wind. I imagined it slowing down, dissipating. I pictured the snow lessening to a light dusting, then stopping entirely. I shook my head. Who was I kidding?

Then a sharp cry from Grey. He staggered back to me from the other side of the fire, his face ashen. He dropped heavily to the ground by my side. I wanted desperately to ask what was wrong, but he didn't seem able to speak. He stared blankly at the fire for a moment, then slumped back down in exhaustion. He just lay there, and I pushed the blankets over him. Chase crawled in under the covers. That seemed to be a good idea. I slipped under the blankets myself and lay along Grey's side, trying to help keep him warm. He shivered intermittently. I nestled closer and put an arm over his chest.

He snuggled closer to me. Chase whimpered and pushed his nose under my hand as if for reassurance.

I lay there, trying to figure out what could have happened. If only I'd been paying attention to Grey instead of concentrating on myself. The only sound was the snapping of the flames and an occasional snort or stamp from Hallin, who stood nearby, head down in dejection. Poor horse; he hadn't been fed and there was nothing I could do about it.

Over the next hours I tried unsuccessfully to doze, and I tended the fire as best I could. It got dark soon and quickly, and I feared the blizzard was getting worse.

The night passed slowly, and Grey didn't stir at all. He seemed to be unconscious rather than asleep. If he was, we were definitely in trouble. I couldn't even get food out of the packs, much less care for a sick man. And as for trying to find help, that would be impossible.

Eventually I managed to fall asleep. Only moments later, it seemed, Grey stirred, and I snapped awake. His head turned from side to side, and he made small moaning noises. I arose and piled more wood onto the fire.

The sky was brightening, so dawn couldn't be far off.

I returned to Grey's side to find him watching me. He looked exhausted, but at least he was conscious now.

"Donavah, you're still here," he said weakly.

I nodded, wondering what he meant. He rubbed the bridge of his nose with his left hand. I wished I could make him some tea—and I could have used some myself. He sat up, stroking Chase's head and looking up at me.

"It must have been a dream. This storm. I . . ." He took a deep breath and let it out again. Then he shook his head as if the physical motion could help clear his thoughts. "I don't know. It was very strange. But it's passed now."

As he shook his head again, I realized that the wind had stopped blowing. And it had stopped snowing. How had I failed to notice that before?

"We need to get moving." Grey rose gingerly to his feet, as if every muscle in his body hurt. I wanted to tell him that we should wait, let him regain some strength, rest a little longer. But the alphabet cloth was still stashed in his pack. Instead, he got the cooking things out and went about making herb tea, putting more sweetening than usual into his cup. I smiled at the realization that I'd become familiar with at least some of his habits in the time we'd been together.

Soon, we were on our way again. Grey held a much slower pace than he had before, and I wondered how long he'd be able to keep going.

As we went eastward through the day, I discovered that the low, dark cloud bank I'd glimpsed several times through the trees was actually the mountains. I swallowed. How would I ever find Xyla and the others? Maybe if I still had my maejic. But I didn't. Before long, Grey would ask me where we were going. And I would have to admit that I didn't know, that I'd let him bring me all this way, in this horrible weather, on a wild goose chase.

Just then, a huge raven swooped down on us, startling Hallin out of his steady plod and causing Chase to start barking wildly. The horse reared up, pawing at the bird, which circled overhead cawing. With no way to hold onto anything, I slid backwards off Hallin's rump, landing with a thud that knocked the breath out of me. I tried to scramble away from the horse's thrashing hooves, but one of them caught my ankle.

Grey struggled to bring Hallin under control, his shouts echoing through the woods, while the bird kept up its raucous noise. He must have decided that the horse wouldn't settle until the bird was gone, because the next thing I knew, he was roundly cursing the raven. It landed on a branch and gave a funny, surprised-sounding chirp, staring at Grey and twitching its head from side to side. Despite the pain in my ankle, I almost laughed.

He shot the bird a very nasty look, then led Hallin in the opposite direction to try to calm him down. As if satisfied with the havoc it had wreaked, the raven let out a last loud cry and flew away.

Then Grey let out another stream of cursing. I looked over to find that Hallin was limping, favoring one of his front legs. Grey examined it and shook his head at what he found. He led the horse back to where I still sat in the snow.

"We have a problem," he said. "He has a strained fetlock. He can walk all right, but he won't be able to carry you."

My heart sank. I had no idea how much farther we had to go, not knowing, after all, where exactly we were actually going. But it didn't matter. If Hallin was hurt and I had to go afoot, then afoot I would go. I looked at Grey, gave him a small smile, and nodded. Then I stood up. Or tried to.

As soon as I put pressure on my right foot, pain shot up my leg. I fell back heavily, tears springing to my eyes. Grey scowled in concern.

"What now?" He knelt next to me and examined my ankle. The air on my exposed skin was cold, but Grey's touch was gentle and warm as he poked and prodded and turned my foot this way and that. He watched my face for reaction, since I couldn't tell him when it hurt. And nothing did hurt until he checked my calf. A searing pain jolted through my leg. I winced and would've cried out if I could have. He tugged up the hem of my trouser leg and frowned at what he saw.

"Well, the good news is that it's not a broken bone or a sprained ankle. Hallin must've gotten you when he was thrashing around. See, the bruise is already coming up." He sighed. "We won't be going any farther today."

Grey went to start gathering firewood, but a few minutes later he returned, a huge smile on his face.

"I've found a great place to camp for the night! We just might stay there two nights—let you and Hallin mend a little before we move on. You stay here while I set a few things up. I'll come back for you." He picked up one of the saddle bags.

I shook my head and rolled my eyes at his departing figure: as if I could go anywhere anyway. What a comic.

It couldn't have been more than twenty minutes before Grey returned, although I'd grown so cold that it seemed like it had been hours. Chase dashed up, wagging his tail and practically dancing.

Grey picked me up as if I weighed little more than a sack of flour. "Just wait'll you see this," he said with a boyish grin.

I couldn't help but smile myself at the childlike glint in his eye, as if he'd done some silly thing that he felt proud of even though he shouldn't.

We hadn't gone far when he said, "There, look."

I had to admit he was right. It really was the perfect place. A space about six feet by eight was enclosed on three sides by huge boulders, and rising from the center was a tall tree. It looked as if the boulders had fallen there from some ancient landslide, the power of the tree stopping them and holding them in place ever since. Grey had used an oilcloth to cover half the shelter in case of rain or more snow, and a fire crackled in front.

He set me down by the fire, and I stretched out my hands toward it. By the time Grey returned with the horse and the rest of the supplies, feeling had started to return.

Soon, Hallin stood in the back of the shelter, eating contentedly from his nosebag and swishing his tail back and forth from time to time. Chase lay curled up next to me, head in my lap as I stroked him with my fist. And supper simmered on the fire. Strictly speaking, it was much too early for supper, but after everything that had happened—the storm, Grey's inexplicable collapse, Hallin's disastrous reaction to the raven—a good, hot meal followed by a long night's sleep seemed to be the most sensible course to follow.

Since it was so early, Grey let the stew simmer longer than usual, and when we finally ate it, the meat was as tender as Mama's best. It made me long for the days when events as well as meals were predictable. A little dullness, with the occasional practical joke from Breyard, would be welcome right now.

I looked at Grey to find him staring into the flames. I wondered what he was thinking about. Probably looking forward to getting me off his hands. As if he felt me watching him, he looked up.

"Ready to sleep?"

I almost nodded, more out of habit than anything else, but really it was still quite early, so I shook my head instead. Then I tried to convey with my eyes how grateful I was for everything he'd done for me. Chase sat up, and I heard his tail thumping on the ground.

Grey's eyes widened a little, and to my surprise, he stood up and walked around the fire, gazing all the time into my eyes. He sat down close to me. His nearness made my heart beat faster, and for the first time, I noticed his earthy odor. I looked at him again and saw an unexpected tenderness deep in his grey eyes. He wore a half smile, and suddenly I wanted him to kiss me, to feel the softness of his lips on mine.

He placed an arm around my shoulders, and I caught my breath. Could this really be happening, or was I dreaming? He pulled me close and leaned his head down toward mine. I closed my eyes and leaned toward him. A thrill went through me as our lips touched and his fingertips brushed my cheek. But at that instant, Hallin screamed in terror.

✦

My patience with King Erno wears thin, and I wonder. Is it because I grow older, for I'm older than the rivers it seems at times. Or is it because the end of the game is at hand, and I anticipate relieving myself of the burden that is the king? Or is it simply that he is, indeed, getting worse?

It matters not, for the wheels are set inexorably in motion, and not even I myself could stop them now.

I gaze into the fire; I sip my tea. I am well pleased.

ThiRTEEN

✦

Chase leapt to his feet, and ran past the fire, barking violently. Grey dashed to Hallin's side, grabbed the horse's bridle, and spoke softly to calm him. I sat in total confusion, trying to pull my cloak closer around my shoulders, almost as if I hoped it could hide me.

Then, as suddenly as they'd started up, both animals stopped. Hallin stood quietly in place, although his eyes were wide with fear. Chase ran to Grey, tail between his legs and whining softly.

I met Grey's eyes, and the expression on his face matched the question in my mind: What was going on? Grey quickly tied Hallin's reins to the tree trunk, loosened two of his knives in their sheaths, and picked up his bow, all without making a sound. As he strung the bow and nocked an arrow, always peering into the darkness beyond the fire, I wished I could do more than stare. He made a quick downward motion with one hand, which I interpreted to mean he didn't want me to move, but he needn't have worried. I was frozen in place.

A current passed through the air. At first I thought it was the wind, but then I noticed that it hadn't affected the flames of the fire. Anazian! It must be. He'd hunted us down and now had us cornered. How could I ever have thought this would be a safe place? Now it looked like nothing but a trap.

I heard harsh breathing and realized it was mine. I put the back of my hand to my mouth and concentrated on taking slow, deep breaths. Anazian could kill me if that's what he wanted to do, but I wasn't going to let him see my fear.

Snow crunched under boots as someone approached. Whoever it was, they certainly weren't bothering to be quiet. A moment later, a shadowy figure emerged from the trees beyond the fire. Grey drew his bow.

A bark of laughter. Then a familiar voice spoke. "That bow does not have the power to kill me, boy."

I jumped to my feet and limped toward Grey. Yallick! How in the world had he found me? He strode into the firelight, Grey's arrow still aimed at his heart. I touched Grey's shoulder. When he glanced at me, I shook my head, and he lowered the weapon. But he remained alert and wary.

"Donavah." Yallick spoke my name with an intense relief.

I just looked at him. He wore buckskin and a heavy black cloak, and his hair was secured back away from his face instead of loose like he usually wore it. But what was most different was his face. He looked much older than he had when I'd last seen him.

"Donavah," Yallick said again, and now he'd come close enough to grip my shoulders in his hands. I saw worry in his eyes.

"She can't speak." Grey's voice was low, and I heard a note of warning in it. Yallick must have, too, because he released me and moved toward Grey.

His gravelly voice low and threatening, Yallick asked, "What have you done to her?"

Grey held his ground, and his eyes narrowed as he glared at Yallick. "I've done nothing but save her life," he growled.

The two men—one young, one old—stared at each other. I stepped between them, placing a fist on each of their chests. This was neither the time nor the place for a misunderstanding.

Yallick was the first to break eye contact, suddenly looking at my hand. With a sharp intake of breath, he grasped my wrist, then reached for the other one. He tried, as Grey had done before, to pry my fingers free, and had the same lack of success. Then he pushed me gently behind him and moved toward Grey again.

"When I find out what you have done—" He was cut off by a loud trumpeting sound.

Xyla!

Without thinking what I was doing, I ran from the shelter, past the fire, and into the woods beyond. Where was she? My only thought was to find the dragon, to be close to her again. Another call, softer this time, placed her straight ahead and not far.

I moved quickly through the trees, heedless of the pain in my leg. I was impatient to find her, to feel her soft hide, to press my face against her and hear the slow rhythm of her heart. To know that she was near me. She'd saved me so many times already that I simply knew everything would be all right again once we were reunited.

I'd scarcely thought of her while we'd been apart, and yet her absence, I realized now, had been unsettling, one of the reasons I couldn't really keep the fear at bay.

And then, there she was. Waiting for me in a clearing barely big enough to contain her. She looked twice the size I remembered.

I stopped at the edge of the trees and just gazed at her. The bright moonlight gleamed off her scales, making it look as if her skin were jewel-encrusted. The tip of her tail twitched ever so slightly, like a sleeping cat's. And her eyes. She looked at me with those deep, wise eyes whose color I was never sure of.

"Xyla!" I tried to call out to her mentally. But there was nothing.

I ran to her. Stretching out my arms wide, I leaned against her. I wept at my inability to hear her, and my tears slid down her skin like diamonds. She reached her head around and rested her chin gently on my head.

I don't know how long we'd stood there when Yallick and Grey approached. I turned around to face them, not caring if they saw my damp cheeks.

"Grey has told me the gist of your—his—story," Yallick said. He laid a bundle on the ground next to me. "I need to get you to our hiding place right away. Let us go."

I looked at Grey, expecting to see him carrying his own pack. Surely he was coming, too. But he only had a heavy fur. He held back a little, staring at the dragon with a look of awe on his face.

"I can't go with you," he finally said, and I heard a note of bitterness in his voice. "Can't take a dog and a horse on . . . you know, a dragon." He swallowed and walked closer. I looked at Xyla in confusion, then back at Grey. "I, well, maybe I'll catch up with you later. Here." He wrapped the fur around me and clipped it in place. "You'll need this. Take good care of yourself."

I couldn't believe that he was just letting me go like this, barely saying goodbye. I looked at Yallick as if to ask him to make Grey come with us, but he was watching me closely with a deep frown on his face. Unable to say anything, all I could do was watch Grey walk away.

"We must be getting back now." Yallick looked at me, then up at Xyla. Unable to use my hands, how would I ever manage to climb up onto her back? Hope rose in my heart at the thought that Yallick would have to call Grey back to help.

Then Xyla seemed to be shrinking, her back getting lower and lower. How could that be? Unless . . . I looked down to find several feet of air between my feet and the ground. Yallick's eyes were closed in concentration, and his right hand moved ever so slightly.

Startled at finding myself floating in midair, I lost my balance. I braced myself for a collision with the ground, but nothing happened; I just floated there at an awkward angle. A tiny movement of Yallick's fingers, and I moved toward Xyla. As soon as she was in reach, I grabbed at her neck and pulled myself onto her back. I sat there breathing heavily, trying to regain my equilibrium. Xyla moved a little, and I started to slide off. Then someone grabbed my shoulders from behind and set me right. I whipped my head around to see who it could be.

"A bit unnerving the first time," Yallick said with a smile. "I apologize."

I might have believed him to be sorry if he'd actually sounded more sincere. Then he levitated the large bundle up, secured it to his back with some rope, and put his arms around my waist.

"Must not have you falling off mid-flight," he said, and I couldn't believe that he was actually laughing. I just stared straight ahead.

Xyla gathered herself and launched into the air. My head snapped back and smashed against Yallick's chin. A muffled cry of pain suggested that perhaps I'd gotten some revenge.

Despite the cold, it felt wonderful to be flying through the night sky on Xyla's back once again. The moon rode high in the sky, and I could see for miles and miles. We headed straight for the jagged skyline that must be the mountains.

I shivered, and Yallick held me tighter, as if to try to warm me. But the joy of being with Xyla again, even if I couldn't hear her, filled my heart and made it easy to ignore the cold. Now that we were together, everything would be all right. I felt as if one of the missing pieces of myself had been put back into place.

Finally, Xyla began to descend. The black ground came closer and closer, and soon I could distinguish the texture of the land below. Dark shadows on the landscape turned into valleys, and ribbons of reflected moonlight must be rivers.

Xyla veered to the left, and I lost my balance. Yallick held me tightly as he leaned into the turn.

Then, even worse, we dropped abruptly. My stomach jumped to my throat as we plummeted. A moment later, Xyla landed delicately on the ground in a large clearing, almost as if she were carrying something fragile.

Immediately, a figure separated from the shadows of the trees.

"Xyla says you have had success." Oleeda! How could she be here? She was supposed to have gone to Roylinn Academy.

"Yes, I have recovered her. But we have a problem."

"Problem?" Oleeda's voice quavered.

"Yes. Come close so I can hand Donavah down to you." Yallick lifted me off Xyla's back and guided me as I slid down the dragon's shoulder. Oleeda reached up to slow my descent, then helped me steady myself once I got to the ground. Yallick threw the bundle down, and a moment later he landed next to me with a soft thud.

"Come." He put an arm around my shoulder and led me toward a glow on the hillside. I limped stiffly at his side. Soon I saw that the glow came from the opening to a cave with a fire burning inside. As we drew nearer, I discovered that the mouth of the cave was huge, much bigger than I first thought, and when Xyla followed us inside, I realized just how vast a cavern it must be.

I stopped at the side of the fire and held out my hands to warm them. I hadn't noticed how numb they'd gotten in the cold until they started to thaw. The feeling of pins and needles brought tears to my eyes, and I stepped back from the fire.

One side of the cave had been made into a comfortable wallow for Xyla, while the other seemed to be set up as living quarters for people. There were several crudely made chairs that must've been built after the arrival of the mages here.

There were also sleeping pallets covered with heavy blankets and furs, and a small body curled up on one of them could only be Traz.

Traz! I hadn't even missed him until this very moment. I wished he were awake. I knew he'd laugh at me, and his jokes would surely put everything into perspective.

He turned over in his sleep, and I hoped he'd wake up, but he just let out a short breath and snuggled deeper under the covers.

And in that moment, I knew why he wanted to become maejic. Having had it and lost it, I now understood how Traz must feel, with everyone around him able to talk to Xyla when he couldn't. And now, neither could I. It had been bad enough during my time with Grey, knowing I'd lost the gift I'd had since before I even knew what it was. But being so near to the mages and—worse in its own way—Xyla made me feel the loss deep in the pit of my stomach.

Yallick had had such hope for me, and now my life was as useless as my hands.

What had been frustrating suddenly became unbearable. Surely there was nothing for me here. Why had Yallick even sought me out? I didn't care how he'd found me; I only wished he hadn't.

Yallick and Oleeda stood near Xyla, their heads close together as if in urgent consultation. Yallick shook his head, and Oleeda put a hand to her mouth, her gasp echoing in the cave.

Suddenly, I couldn't stand to be near these people who had all their mysterious plans and even more mysterious powers. Why had I ever thought to seek them out? I would have been better off staying with Grey, who didn't have grand plans for my life—plans that now could never be fulfilled. But Grey didn't really want me to be with him, either. He'd wanted to get rid of me.

Escape! That's what I needed to do. Get far, far away where they'd never find me.

No one was watching me as I moved toward the cave entrance. How far could I go before they'd notice I'd gone? Before I'd be too cold to keep moving? That's all the time I needed, because then I would die quickly. With any luck, it wouldn't hurt much. Nothing like the pain I felt right now.

Then I was outside, running. Running as fast as I could to get far away. To find a quiet place to curl up and sleep. Forever.

✦

I have found Donavah, but I cannot say she is safe and sound. Some hideous spell has been laid upon her, one of grave and frightening power. If, that is, her companion is to be believed. She did not contradict him, so it must be true, or at least something that she, too, believes to be the truth. She cannot speak to tell me what has happened.

At least she is now back in my care. If I can care for her. I fear that the healing is beyond my skill.

For what reason was she brought to me in the first place, if only to be damaged so irreparably? No, I cannot allow myself the luxury of raillery.

Oleeda has joined us. Perhaps together we will have enough power to do that which neither of us could hope to do alone. Perhaps.

Fourteen

I didn't get far. A loud trumpeting from Xyla pierced the night air, and running footsteps came after me. I couldn't go any faster with the pain in my leg. Yallick caught up with me and grabbed my arm, forcing me to stop. He didn't speak a word as he turned me around and marched me back to the cave.

Once inside, he grasped my upper arms tightly and looked into my eyes. I tried to look away, but it was as if he'd laid some kind of compulsion on me. My eyes filled with tears of shame that spilled down my cheeks. And still his blue-green eyes bore into mine. Then he blinked.

He wrapped me in a bear hug, stroking my hair gently. That broke the dam inside me, and I found myself once again weeping as I had that once with Grey—uncontrollable, bone-rattling sobs that yet made no noise.

"The strain," Yallick said in a soft voice, almost a whisper. "You are terribly confused. More, I think, than you realize."

"Not exactly a surprise." I felt Oleeda's hands gently kneading my shoulders. "We do not yet know all that she has been through. We should try the healing now."

I pulled away from Yallick. *Try?* What did she mean, *try?*

Yallick's eyes narrowed in concentration. "No. Not yet. All three of us must husband our strength, Donavah most of all." He placed an arm around my shoulders. "Come. Sleep now," he said, leading me toward the pallets where Traz lay still sound asleep.

I bent down and scooped up the covers in my arms. Yallick watched, a concerned frown furrowing his brow, as I stalked over to Xyla. She gave a small snort—in amusement, it seemed—as I settled myself between her front legs, as if they were a nest built solely for my comfort.

As if Oleeda understood my need to assert myself, even if only in this small way, she shushed Yallick when he started to object. I watched them move closer to the fire and sit down. Oleeda poured cups of what must be herb tea, and they began to speak softly. I couldn't distinguish words, and soon the solemn, even tone of their voices lulled me to sleep.

+ + +

Where I dreamed of being Queen. I had the power of life and death over everyone, from the lowliest serving child to the greatest nobles and magicians in the land. All quaked before my wrath. Men from beyond the waters sought my hand in marriage, and I joyed in spurning them all. I hosted lavish entertainments where knights wrestled, raced, fenced, and sparred for my attention; where the orchestra played until dawn as all danced at my command; where we feasted, and laughed, and drank, and sang. But never hunted.

+ + +

I awoke to find Traz standing over me, hands on hips and an exaggerated scowl on his face.

"I can't believe you didn't wake me up last night," he said, and despite the pout he wore, there was a giggle in his voice.

I pushed myself up and rubbed my eyes with my fists. I started to smile at him, then broke into a huge yawn. Daylight poured into the cave. I'd slept a long time, but strange dreams had prevented me from getting any real rest.

"It's been very dull hanging around with ol' Yallick, so you'd better start telling me everything about your adventures right away."

"Your impertinence will avail you nothing," Yallick said from the table, where he was ladling porridge into a bowl.

Traz rolled his eyes, and I grinned. Say what they might to and about each other, I could sense that somehow, they'd grown attached to one another.

"Come, Donavah," Yallick continued. "You must eat now to build up your strength."

I climbed out of my makeshift bed. The air in the cavern was cold, despite the roaring fire near the front, and I shivered. Traz and I walked over to the table and sat down.

"So, tell me everything," Traz demanded again as he poured tea into a cup. "I want to hear every detail." He sipped at the tea and looked at me expectantly.

I didn't know what to do. I couldn't tell him what had happened, and Yallick didn't seem inclined to do so for me. Oleeda would surely have come to the rescue, but she wasn't here. In the end I just shrugged, looked away, and picked up my bowl between my still-clenched fists.

As the porridge slid down my throat, it had the strange effect of making me feel hungrier. I hadn't been eating a lot lately, but neither had I been starving myself. I practically drank down the whole lot, and I'd scarcely set the bowl on the table before Yallick spooned more into it.

When I picked up the bowl the second time, I found Traz staring at my hands with a hurt expression on his face. I very much wanted to explain, but, unaccountably, even more I wanted to eat. After a third helping, Yallick muttered, "Worked even better than I expected."

I set the bowl down heavily and scowled at him.

"Well," he shrugged and turned away, "I needed to make sure you would eat."

I would have thrown something at him if I could have been certain it would've hit him. Then . . .

"Nobody ever tells me anything!" Traz shouted, jumping to his feet. "I hate you all!" And he went tearing out of the cave without even picking up his cloak. I rose to go after him, but Yallick stopped me.

"You eat some more. I will take care of our young friend."

I tried to do as he told me, but my stomach was now so full that I couldn't force down another mouthful, no matter what kind of spell Yallick had mixed into the food.

When they returned about ten minutes later, Yallick had obviously told Traz what had happened. Well, as much of it as he knew, anyway. Or cared to share.

Traz sat back down. "Sorry, Donavah," he muttered, looking embarrassed. I smiled and reached across the table to tousle his hair with my fist. He gave me a shy smile back.

Oleeda walked in then, carrying several bundles of herbs. "I think I found everything we need," she said, striding toward the rear of the cave. "Did she eat?"

"She did," Yallick said. "I made sure of it."

A flash of anger rose up inside me, but I forced it down.

Traz hastily gulped his breakfast, gathered his cloak and staff, and made ready to leave. "I hope it all goes well. And you, old man," he said, as he passed Yallick on his way out, "you take care of her."

"I will, Traz." Yallick spoke surprisingly gently. "You may trust that I will."

Their eyes locked for a moment, then Traz nodded once, turned, and left. When he was gone, Yallick sat at the table with me.

"Oleeda and I have much to do to prepare. A powerful spell like this—" he pointed at my hands, "—requires an even more powerful counterspell. We must concentrate on what we do." He paused, as if he expected some kind of response, so I nodded. "This will be an ordeal for all of us, Donavah. I will be honest with you and say that I do not know what to expect. But we must try. Do you trust us?"

I considered. If he and Oleeda had no idea what to expect, I had even less. Trust didn't seem to be much of an issue. I couldn't live the rest of my life like this, could I? I must let them try and hope they would succeed. Things couldn't get worse. I nodded solemnly.

"That is good. Stay by the fire to keep warm. And be patient. This will take time."

About that, he wasn't kidding. I sat with the fire behind me, watching Yallick and Oleeda prepare. Xyla lay stretched out along the side of the cave seemingly intent on the dance that the two mages wove.

Oleeda placed candles in a circle, then examined her work. She moved one slightly to the left, another a bit back, yet another farther in, until she was satisfied that they were perfectly situated. Meanwhile, Yallick scratched a complicated design into the dirt floor. Back and forth, round and round. They moved with a rhythm that seemed unconscious.

Eventually, when I began to wonder what more they could possibly need to do, Yallick came to me. First he pulled a small branch from the fire, then he took my hand and led me to the circle.

Oleeda took the branch and moved around the circle lighting the tapers. There was one of each color of meditation candle. Yallick chanted in a language that I didn't understand at first but soon recognized as Zahrainian, which I'd studied back at Roylinn. "Power," "light," and "life" were several of the words I thought I picked out of the unfamiliar stream.

When Oleeda had completed the circuit and all the candles were burning brightly, she stood next to me and joined Yallick in the chant.

Then he went around the circle in the opposite direction, dropping a pinch of powder onto each flame. The powder ignited with a small pop and released an odor that was an unidentifiable mix of herbs. By the time he returned to my side, the air was thick and fragrant.

Yallick stepped into the circle, reached for my hand, and drew me in. He positioned me in the exact center and stood behind me.

The cave went quiet as he and Oleeda stopped chanting, the only noise an occasional snap from the fire. Oleeda went around the circle dropping more of the powder onto the candles. Yallick took my hands in his and raised them until my arms were straight out to my sides. He began to chant again while Oleeda made yet another round with the powder.

It grew hard to breathe. I took huge gulps of air and choked on the fumes.

Then a searing pain burst through me from the top of my head to my hands and toes. If it were possible, I would have screamed. It felt as if I'd been struck by lightning. I began to lose consciousness as wave upon wave of pain rolled through my body. And yet I stood rooted to the spot, unable even to fall down. My muscles contracted, and I could no longer breathe at all. My hair felt as if it were standing out on end. My heart stopped beating.

And I found myself floating comfortably in the air, looking down on a miasma of swirling colors. Yallick, Oleeda, and my body began to spin, melting into the fog of color. The mages both cried out in pain and collapsed. My body stood stiff, held up by a power I could never hope to understand.

Xyla trumpeted. Then again. And yet again. The sound echoed off the walls of the cave and tore through my head.

Two mages came running in. I watched as they raced to the three figures below me. One went to Oleeda and stooped over her; the other stood looking back and forth from my upright body to Yallick's crumpled form. Yallick stirred just as the mage reached toward me.

"No," Yallick moaned, but it was too late. The mage touched my arm, and my body crashed to the floor.

✦

My son sits poised like a spider on its web. The fly is wary, sensing the predator nearby, but not yet grasping that it is trapped. Soon, soon it will discover the truth.

All that is left is to spring the trap at just the right moment, when the prey thinks himself strong yet is indeed most vulnerable.

Patience. The final play will come soon, but not quite yet.

Fifteen

Someone was moving me, and I wished they wouldn't. My brain whirled inside my skull, and if it didn't stop soon, I would vomit.

Then, stillness. Furs were placed over me and tucked in.

"Is she . . . ?" a woman's shaky voice whispered.

"She breathes. She lives." A gravelly male voice drained of any vitality.

A gentle hand on my forehead. A voice I couldn't place murmuring soft words. I fell into a deep sleep.

+ + +

I lay there, lethargic, unmoving, and barely conscious for I don't know how long. I felt no pain, and for that I was thankful, but neither did I feel anything else. It was as if I were paralyzed, mind, body, and spirit.

Eventually, I remembered who I was. Soon after that, I remembered where I was and some vague ideas about how I'd gotten here. But somehow, none of it mattered. All I cared about was never, ever, moving again.

Sometimes, I caught snippets of conversation.

"Stop blaming yourself, Yallick." A snort. "This bout of self-pity is not doing Donavah any good. Or you."

"We should not have rushed. We did not know what we were dealing with. She might never . . ." He broke off, and the anguish in his voice almost brought a tear to my eye. Almost.

"When she is stronger, we will try again. We will just go more carefully."

Yallick sighed. "I only wish we knew what happened, what we are up against, what we need to do."

"Me, too," Oleeda said.

I thought to open my eyes, but couldn't be bothered just then.

+ + +

A cool hand took up one of mine. It felt good.

"Donavah." It was Yallick. "Donavah. Wherever you are, come back to us. We need you. We want you back."

Need me? Want me? What did I need? What did I want? I needed a drink, and I wanted to stay warm. Safe. Protected.

I opened my eyes.

"Donavah!" Yallick leaned over me. His face was haggard and grey, with dark circles under eyes that were too tired to shine with their usual brilliance. He looked older than I'd ever seen him, almost his real age.

"Oleeda!" He almost hissed her name. "She stirs!"

Sounds of movement, then Oleeda's face came into view, looking almost as bad as Yallick's. She gently stroked my hair, a tender smile on her lips.

"How are you, dear?"

No way to say anything. No desire to, either. I just lay there, content with things as they were.

Oleeda lifted a cup and tried to get me to drink. A few drops spilled onto my tongue. A healing infusion of thyme, hyssop, wild lavender, and more. How did I know that? Everything was too confusing. I swallowed, closed my eyes, and fell back to sleep.

+ + +

Vague memories of Oleeda and Yallick trying to coax me into swallowing more of their remedies. Sometimes I cooperated, other times I didn't. Still nothing made sense. My concept of myself kept slipping in and out of focus.

+ + +

I opened my eyes to find Traz staring at me. He gave me an impudent grin.

"You're awake! Yallick and Oleeda left me to watch. They said you wouldn't wake up, but I knew you would if I could just get the words right."

I felt him lift something that had been lying across my chest. His staff.

"So, I know you can't tell me about your adventures, but if you want, I can tell you about ours. I mean, after that night of the attack."

He took my non-response as affirmative and plunged into his tale.

"So first there was that lightning. It was everywhere. I got blinded by it, and I couldn't find you. In all the confusion, I managed to make my way to Yallick. I thought you would, too." A long pause. He touched my cheek. "I wish you had." And there was nothing I could say.

"Anyway, it was total chaos. People getting struck and killed by lightning, everyone scattering. The next morning, we regrouped, found out just how bad it was. About half the mages were either dead or missing, and a lot were hurt, too." He paused again, and I could tell he was struggling with tears. Finally he swallowed the lump in his throat, blinked his eyes, and went on.

"Some of the mages wanted to move on right away, but Yallick said we had to stay there for at least a few days. Because of the injured people, you know. And also in case anyone missing tried to find us. He said once we'd gone, they'd be on their own.

"The mages who were left cast these spells to keep us hidden, and I guess it worked, because we didn't get attacked again."

Something fell into place. The dragonmasters had always known where the group was when Anazian was part of it. *He* must be the one who . . . but what connection could he possibly have with the dragonmasters?

"After a few days, Yallick finally decided that we'd best be on our way. It was slow going, with so many people still hurt. A few even had to be carried on litters. It was dismal. No one talked, and we had to eat our food cold. At night we had fires, but that meant extra mages had to keep watch to maintain the hiding spells. And everyone was tired and exhausted all the time.

"We made our way to the mountains, slowly but surely. Yallick was getting birds from Xyla, so he knew exactly where to go. But he was worried sick, Donavah. For everyone, of course, but mostly for you.

"Then we got here. This place is great! Just wait 'til you see. There are caves all around this valley. I don't know how Xyla found it, but it's perfect. Everyone divided up into small groups. Yallick made me stay with him." I almost smiled when Traz curled his lip at that. "Every day, Yallick and I rode out on Xyla trying to find you. And any of the others. That's how we found Oleeda. She'd heard about what happened and was coming as fast as she could.

"It was just awful when Xyla couldn't find any trace of you anywhere. Yallick got so irritable that I was half-tempted to run away. Then finally, that raven came back with word that he thought he'd found you. You wouldn't believe how fast Yallick and Xyla tore out of here. He wouldn't have remembered his cloak if Oleeda hadn't . . ." He stopped mid-sentence and looked toward the entrance to the cave. The expression on his face quickly changed, and I guessed that Yallick and Oleeda must have returned.

I felt him slip his staff under the fur, and he whispered, "I'll get it back soon." Then he stood up straight.

"She's waking up. I told you she would."

I heard Yallick guffaw. Soon Oleeda was at my side administering yet another of her potions. This time, I accepted it readily, and this surprised her. With a tiny pang, I realized that I'd not been a very easy patient. She actually smiled when the last of the drink had safely gone down my throat.

"I think she's improving," she said, rising to her feet. Then her face fell, and I wondered what made her so sad. It must be all those people dead and missing that Traz had told me about.

+ + +

Later, I don't know how many hours or days, Yallick came and sat on the pallet, shifting my legs aside to give himself enough room to sit. He held my hand in his for the longest time. Some of the warmth from his hands even seemed to seep into my arm muscles. Then he reached up and brushed my cheek with the back of his fingers.

"My child." His voice was barely above a whisper. "My little one. Please come back to us. We miss you. We need you." He took a deep breath and let it out in a long sigh. "I do not know what to do for you, my dear. You must find it in yourself. I know it is hard. Harder, I think, than anything I have ever had to do. But you are strong. Dig deep, child, and find what is necessary. We are here. We are waiting."

He stopped speaking and just looked into my eyes. His own eyes had regained some of their brightness, and I fancied that I saw them sparkle in the firelight. Then I realized it was tears.

Yallick weeping for me? I almost felt like laughing. He liked nothing better than to make me miserable. He taught me many things, that was true, but it wasn't because it was what he wanted to do. No, he felt under some compulsion, some duty. But as I watched him watching me, I couldn't deny that he cared. What a strange idea. I tried to reconcile it with the ill-tempered mage who drilled his lessons into me.

I heard someone enter the cave. Yallick quickly wiped his eyes. I felt the twinge of a smile, the first in forever, it seemed.

"Someone is coming toward the camp!" Oleeda said.

Instantly, my heart began to race. They'd found us! They would attack again, and this time, we were all trapped. They would capture Xyla, make her fight in the pits. Everything that had happened would be for nothing, absolutely nothing.

Yallick stood up. "Who?"

"The watch is not sure yet. Janel said it looked like just one person. I feel no fear from the forest. Perhaps it is another mage."

Yallick nodded. "It could be." I could see some of the tension in his body relax. So he'd been as frightened as I. "Word does indeed seem to be getting out. More rejoin us every day."

Then I heard voices—happy voices—shouting outside the cave. Yallick must be right. It must be one of the missing mages. More people came into the cave. I turned my head slightly to try to see. The excitement in the air was palpable, even to me.

Yallick's face lit up in pleasure, and he dashed away from my side.

"It *is* you!" he almost shouted. "I had thought you surely lost, man. Not a single bird brought back word of you."

"I was not lost, my old friend, only misplaced." His booming laugh bounced off the cave walls.

Anazian.

✦

More mages arrive every day. Perhaps our losses are not so dire
as I first believed. As our number increases, so does our power.

It has been weeks since the last attack. Have we
escaped? It is said that no news is good news, and there has
been no news. All is quiet for many miles around.

But I grieve for Donavah. She lingers away. Would
death be better than this lethargy that smothers her spirit?
I dare not meddle further.

Sixteen

That night, when everyone was finally asleep, I sat up. My muscles felt like mush. How long had I lain there unmoving? It seemed like it had been only minutes, yet it also seemed like it had been forever.

Slowly, carefully, so as not to make any noise, I slid my feet to the ground. I tried to stand, but my knees shook and I had to sit back down.

Closing my eyes, I forced myself to concentrate. I took a few shuddering breaths before my lungs seemed to get used to the idea, then I breathed deeply, trying to draw vitality from the air. After a few moments, my strength seemed to return.

I rose, and though my movements were awkward from inactivity, it didn't feel as if I would collapse with the next step.

Expecting one of the others to wake up at any moment, I crept to the rear of the cave. Since Yallick and Oleeda always went back there to meditate, I hoped to find some meditation candles.

Sure enough, in the dim light from the fire, I found a large, neat stack of tapers in every color. Concentrating on moving deliberately and quietly, I managed to pick up two candles between my fists, white and turquoise. Then I went outside, where I paused to get my bearings. A full moon shed silver light on the snow-covered ground, broken here and there with tall shrubs and small boulders. Not far away, the woods began in earnest. A faint path of trodden-down snow was the only evidence that humans resided here.

I took a deep breath of the crisp, fresh air. And that's when I noticed that I wasn't cold. Strange, but no time to think about it now. Next to the mouth of the cave was a flat spot, clear of brush and boulders that would suit just fine. I set the candles on the ground and went back inside for more.

When I got to the back of the cave, Traz stood there, arms crossed and lips pursed. He didn't say a word, but his annoyance spoke loud enough almost to wake a sleeping dragon.

I gave him a pleading look that I hoped he could see in the dim light, then moved to the stack of candles and stooped to pick up more. The first one slipped and clattered to the floor, seeming loud in the stillness. I held my breath and looked back toward the place where the others slept. Nothing.

Traz touched my shoulder and whispered, "Let me help." Grateful for the offer, I nodded. He picked up as many as he could carry in both hands, and I followed him outside. He shivered in the cold breeze as he set them on the ground next to the others, then he dashed back inside.

The moonlight was bright enough for me to see clearly, and I was pleased to find that there was at least one candle of every color. I began to arrange them in a circle. I chose the colors randomly, but my movements felt far more sure of themselves than they should have.

Just as I finished my circle, Traz reappeared and went around the circle and made sure each candle stood perfectly upright, packing its base in snow. When he was done, he lit them for me. The breeze died when he lit the first one.

He came over to me, stood on tiptoe to give me a quick kiss on the cheek, then went back inside, still shivering from the cold. Which I didn't feel.

I stepped into my circle and stood unmoving. Then I closed my eyes tightly and tried to find my calm center. At first it was hard. My mind kept wandering back to what had happened, what Anazian had done to me. Earlier in the evening, when Yallick had brought him to my bedside, he'd said nothing but only looked at me with an unreadable expression on his face. That look had sent chills down my spine and convinced me that I had to take responsibility for my own healing. I tried not to think about how arrogant this was, trying to do something that Yallick and Oleeda together, with all their power, had failed to do. I returned my thoughts to Anazian. He had left me once before to die a horrible death, and although he'd failed, I saw now that he'd done something even worse: he'd turned fear into my way of life.

Anger flowed through me. I had no idea of his plans, but I was the only one who could stop him.

And the fear fell from me as I finally, after such a long time, found my calm center. All other thoughts fled, and my mind felt blank. No, not blank, but free.

I breathed. In, out, in, out. Air, the primary sustenance of life. Cleansing, pure, restorative. Filling not just my lungs, but my entire being.

I raised my hands over my head and began to turn in place. With my movements, I created rhythm. Or did I move in the rhythm of the air, the forest, the world? I swayed a little, as if using motion to draw power to myself.

The dance of the universe. Within the bounds of my circle of candlelight, I joined in. A strand of elemental life brushed my cheek, and I brought my hands down to try to capture it.

A thrill of power, almost but not quite painful, ignited inside my head. It set up a pulse in counterpoint to my movements. I held my breath for a moment but continued to move, allowing the forces at play to establish a new flow within me.

Then I stopped and stood quite still. Power sparked in the air all around me. I wanted to reach out and pull it into myself, but I couldn't. I'd been stripped of my maejic. No! I cut off that line of thought. I must simply imagine I could make the maejic work.

In my mind's eye, I wove strands of power into a rope, a lifeline. I allowed myself to sink deep into an unreal world where my hands and voice were again at my command. Where fear held no sway over me. And where my life was my own to live as I chose.

The stars began to sing, and I stretched my hands out to catch the music on my fingertips. The melody coursed through my blood. I sang in harmony.

"You don't really think it's that easy, do you?" The spell broke as Anazian laughed at me.

I fell to the ground in a heap to find that the candles had burned down to nothing more than puddles of colored wax in the snow. Fear blossomed in my heart and stole the air from my lungs. Then I noticed my hands splayed in front of me. Flat, not balled into fists. I sucked in a breath. Pushing myself up, I rose to my feet to face my adversary. I didn't know how much Yallick had told him, but had to assume it was everything. Very well. Let Anazian think I was still afflicted with his curse.

I stood within my circle, breathing hard and staring at the mage.

"Well," he said, a sneer in his voice. "Finding you here was certainly an unwelcome surprise." He took several steps closer to me. I willed myself not to back away. "You thought you had so much power. The way you flaunted it made me sick to my stomach. You can't imagine how much pleasure it brought me to strip you of it. And it was so easy." He laughed again, loudly. My eyes flicked to the cave opening, willing Yallick, Oleeda, even Traz, to come out.

Anazian noticed. "Oh, you think that your master will save you this time? Yallick!" he shouted. "Come out and save your weak, little pet." He looked at the cave and waited. "Oh!" He turned back to me. "Wait. They're not going to wake any time soon. If at all. No, probably not at all. I'm better than that, you see. Even if I did somehow fail to kill you."

He walked around the circle several times. I stared straight ahead and didn't move. He stopped behind me. "Turn and face me."

Instead, I walked out of the circle and into the cave. Yallick, Traz, and Oleeda all lay still on their pallets near the fire. I could scarcely see their chests rising and falling. Anazian was right behind me.

"I do not like being disobeyed, girl. Perhaps I should teach you a lesson in obedience." Then his voice took on a gentle tone that was, if anything, even more sinister than his anger. "But I will allow you this sop, to say goodbye to your useless friends."

I felt Traz's face. It was cold, almost as cold as death. And suddenly I felt as if a fire were burning inside me. Traz was a ten-year-old boy. He'd done nothing to earn Anazian's hatred. He was just an innocent bystander. I spotted his staff next to his pallet. With an unexpected strength, I grabbed it and turned on Anazian, my only thought to beat his head to a pulp.

He wasn't expecting my sudden attack, but even so, he was able to raise an arm in time to deflect the blow.

There seemed to be a hum in the air, intensifying my concentration. It was as if something else were in control of my body. Thrust, parry, thrust again. Anazian had no weapon except maejic, but that was still an effective shield.

He backed away from my wrath, watching the staff in my hands as I tried to bring it down on his head. With first one hand and then the other, he drew power from the air to protect himself as he backed away from my onslaught.

Then we were outside. The staff quickened in my hands, as if the fresh air gave it new vigor. But Anazian, too, seemed to be able to draw on the energy flow all around us. I paused and glanced around. The last thing I needed now was to stumble on the unfamiliar ground.

But that pause was enough for my opponent. He raised his hands over his head, grasping at nothing that I could see.

He shouted an incantation and threw a ball of blue cosmic flame at me.

Instinctively, I raised the staff. The flame hit it and the force of the impact knocked me back several steps. The staff absorbed the flame and began to vibrate. I tried to drop it before it shook my bones free of my flesh, but I couldn't let go.

A loud crack rent the air, and the staff seemed to explode in my hands. Red lightning flew from its tip, following the arc of the flame, right back to Anazian. In the red flash, I saw a look of terror on his face, then I had to look away from the bright light. My hands felt as if they were on fire, and this time when I let go, the staff fell sizzling into the snow. When I could see again, there was no sign of Anazian. Anywhere.

✦

For all my counsel to the contrary, I grow impatient. Such foolishness! What are a few weeks, compared to a plan five hundred years in the making?

The king calls for me now, and I must attend. Having lost one dragon, he fears that our power dwindles. Imbecile! Truly he is unworthy of his title "Absolute Monarch." And yet, maybe I should not be so quick to fault him. He himself has no power and cannot comprehend how it works. I shudder to think what he would be like if he did have power.

Perhaps I shall distract him with a game of Talisman and Queen. Perhaps I shall even let him win.

Seventeen

✦

I picked up the staff and rose to my feet, wary for Anazian's reappearance. I closed my eyes and opened my internal senses. There. The life vibration of the forest flowed through me, welcoming me as a long-lost friend. And without a trace of negative energy. The joy of once again experiencing the maejic almost hurt. I could even feel the subtle consciousness of the sleeping dragon. How would I ever be able to explain everything to Yallick?

Yallick! Oleeda and Traz! I whirled around and ran back into the cave. I dropped Traz's staff and pushed it aside with my foot, then scooped up an armful of wood and threw it onto the fire. I examined all three of them and found them wan and grey. Their breathing grew more shallow every minute. Time was running out.

I tried to think. How could I ever hope to counter another of Anazian's spells? Frustration threatened yet again to overwhelm me.

Yallick's head moved ever so slightly, and he let out a long ragged breath. And didn't take another.

I couldn't just let them die! It was unthinkable that Anazian should have the last word.

Herbs. There had to be something that would help. A large sack lay next to Oleeda's pallet. I wrestled for only a second with the propriety of rummaging through her things without permission. Inside, I found packet after packet of dried herbs—some for strengthening, some for healing, some for calming, and many I couldn't even identify. Which ones to use?

All of them. In my haste to get to the fire, I tripped over the staff. Kicking it aside, I dumped the contents of the bag onto the fire, not worrying about the paper wrappers. They'd burn off quick enough.

Within seconds, the air filled with pungent fumes. I moved back to where the others lay. Oleeda and Traz were still taking intermittent breaths. Yallick lay unmoving.

My mind froze as I tried to force it to think of something, anything. I saw that Traz's staff had fallen across Yallick's knees. Feeling a little guilty, I grabbed it to move it away, and as soon as my fingers touched it, Yallick's entire body heaved upward.

I let out a cry of surprise. Yallick's eyes flew open as he sucked in a great gasp of air. I stared at the staff, wanting and yet not daring to drop it again.

Now sitting up, Yallick let out a groan, then started coughing in the herb-laden atmosphere. I finally managed to uproot myself. I moved first to Oleeda and then to Traz, touching them each with the staff, while Yallick watched in wide-eyed astonishment. Soon, Oleeda and Traz were sitting up, moving for all the world like people awakened from bad dreams.

"What . . . what happened?" Yallick asked, rubbing the back of his neck.

"You all almost died.'" My voice, so long unused, rasped.

Yallick and Oleeda gazed at me with identical expressions of wonder on their faces. Oleeda tried to rise, but fell back as if in exhaustion. Even Xyla stirred in her sleep, though she didn't wake.

"Well, give us the bare bones, at least, and then I think we shall sleep again."

Traz still hadn't spoken, although he watched my every move with staring eyes. He seemed to like the suggestion of sleeping again, and he snuggled back under the covers.

I sighed. What to tell them? I didn't feel sure of anything myself. "Let me make you some tea first," I said, stalling for time. Yallick nodded in agreement.

By now, the air had started to clear. I found a small cooking pot next to the fire, but no water. Well, that was easily solved. There was plenty of clean snow outside.

This time when I stepped out of the cavern, the full cold of the winter night smote me, and I gasped. I looked around for Anazian again, but neither saw nor felt any disturbance in the surrounding woods. The sharp air seemed to burn my lungs, and having got what I was after, I hurried back inside.

As the water heated, I looked around for the rest of the cooking gear. I finally found it on a natural shelf in the rock wall of the cave. Cups, plates, eating utensils, mostly the things we'd carried here with us. That *they'd* carried here. A lump rose unexpectedly in my throat at the thought of my pack. Ridiculous, really, to get worked up over it after all this time. It wasn't as if I'd been carrying anything of real significance. It's just that it seemed to represent lost innocence in some way. I sighed.

I found a large packet of herbs and returned to the fire. As the tea steeped, I breathed a simple incantation over the cups, one to speed both sleep and healing.

Traz weakly batted at my hand, but I insisted that he drink. In the end, I had to pull the furs off him, and that spurred him into gulping the stuff down. He was practically snoring before I finished covering him again.

Oleeda and Yallick took the cups I offered them and drank without speaking. It felt very strange to have switched places so suddenly.

Then there was nothing left to do, and I still hadn't figured out how to explain everything.

"So tell us what happened," Yallick said, scarcely finishing the sentence before yawning. Oleeda had already lain back down, her eyes beginning to droop.

I cleared my throat. Maybe to start with the least complicated part. "Well, the time just seemed right to try to do something for myself. I woke up." I paused and bit my lower lip, then corrected myself. "I was still awake after the rest of you fell asleep. I built the circle of meditation candles . . ." Yallick's soft snore cut me off. In that short time, he and Oleeda had both fallen asleep. I raised my eyebrows in mild surprise. I hadn't expected my incantation to work so quickly.

I went over to Xyla and gently stroked her neck. She let out a soft sigh, and I hoped she would wake up. I couldn't wait to talk to her again, to hear her comforting voice. Even as she slept, though, I could feel some of her power flowing to me as my hand made contact with her skin.

Then, without warning, all of my own energy drained from me. What had happened outside within my circle, I still didn't understand, but among other things, it had given me a boost of vigor. Now that the need was over, though, I felt as tired as the others looked. I went to my pallet and lay down, but my mind kept buzzing and I couldn't sleep. Eventually I got up and made myself some tea, and it worked as well for me as it had for the others.

+ + +

I woke up before dawn, while the others slept on. It didn't look as if any of them had stirred, and they were all breathing normally. I reached out beyond the cave, but found no disturbance in the vibrations. I'd better stay unblocked. I didn't want anyone—least of all Anazian—catching me unawares.

I built up the fire and sat near it, looking at my hands in wonder. It hadn't been a dream! I whispered my name, and the sound of it caressed my ears like a stream over smooth pebbles. Smiling, I hummed a tune, a lullaby I remembered Mama singing to me whenever I was ill as a small child. I picked up small twigs with my fingertips, taking joy from such a simple action. I felt the course nap of the fabric of my tunic, the dirt floor of the cave, the skin of my face. It was almost as if I'd awakened from a very long nightmare to find a sunny, Spring morning shining through the window. A whole new life!

Then all of a sudden, "Donavah?"

"Xyla!" I jumped up and ran to her.

I stopped far enough away that I could take in her full size. She was huge, her belly bulging more than I would have thought possible. She watched me with her lips slightly parted in what I took to be a dragonish smile.

"Xyla," I said again, and it felt good to know that she could hear me again. "I've missed you so much."

"I have been here all along," she said. "You have been here some time, too."

"I know, but I couldn't hear you. It was awful." I walked closer and placed a hand on her shoulder.

"I missed you, too, little one, though I could hear *you*."

I stared up at her. "You could? But how? Anazian took away my maejic."

She blew out a great snort of air. "Surely you do not believe that he could do that?"

"But it was gone. I couldn't hear any animals, couldn't feel vibrations, or anything. It was . . . it was the loneliest I've ever felt."

Xyla curled her long neck around and lay her head on the ground close to me. "It was nothing more than what most people have their whole lives."

That made me stop and think.

"Well, it was still awful. I'm so glad it's over now. But if Anazian didn't take my power away, what happened?"

"The mind is a powerful inhibitor. He had only to make you *think* he had stripped you of your maejic."

"He definitely succeeded at that."

"He is strong. His spell on you was potent, one that took many, many days for him to work. He is a great force with which we must now reckon."

"It took days? He must have been planning it for . . ." I broke off at the enormity of that thought. "But why?"

"It is hard to say. We may never know."

"Well, I'm going to find out. To me, this was personal. Very personal."

"Some of the scars may never heal. But still, you will be stronger."

I guffawed. "I wonder. But that's enough about me. How are you? You've gotten so big!"

"The little ones grow well. The time will be soon."

I grinned in anticipation. "How soon? And after that, how long before the eggs will hatch?" I couldn't wait to see the baby dragons, to hold them and play with them.

Xyla grumbled in that chuckling way she had. "You will see."

A scuffling noise came from behind me. I turned to see Yallick walking stiffly toward us, moving as if every muscle pained him. His long, white-blond hair, unbound again, was dishevelled, and his skin still looked grey.

I moved quickly to his side, ready to lend a steadying hand if he needed it. "Are you all right?"

He place a hand on my shoulder and gave me a weak smile. Peering into my eyes, he nodded.

"Let me make you some more tea," I said.

"No!" he practically barked. "Not another of your potions!"

I couldn't help it: I laughed out loud. And it felt unbearably good to be able to.

"Well, if you think I need to rest easy today, you are right. But I will not do so until you tell me everything that has happened. My powers do not extend to reading minds."

He leaned backward against Xyla and slid to the ground. I sat next to him, both of us using the dragon as a backrest, and told him the full story. It seemed to go on for hours. Eventually Oleeda and Traz awoke and got up, but they didn't approach, as if they knew better than to interrupt us. Well, interrupt me. Yallick didn't say a word through my entire tale. I grew hoarse with the telling; after all, my voice had gone unused for weeks now. When I'd finished, a long silence stretched and grew into a deafening roar. Finally, Yallick broke it.

"And you expect me to believe this?"

Donavah's power has saved me. Saved Oleeda and Traz, as well. And, most importantly, herself. It is a marvel. It takes my breath away to consider it. I become convinced more and more that she, not Xyla, is the "strong one" of the prophecy.

And yet there is this nonsense she tells me about Anazian. It is impossible. Utterly, completely, thoroughly impossible. I fear that what she has endured the past weeks has unhinged her mind, and if this is the case, it is woeful tidings indeed.

Eighteen

My jaw dropped. After everything I'd been through, how dare he not believe me?

Yallick went on before I could say anything. "What you are telling me is that a mage—one whom I myself trained—has become a traitor." His blue-green eyes stared at me, icier than ever before.

"But it's true. I'm telling you the . . ."

"Quiet! Let me think."

I couldn't believe it. He'd seen the results of what Anazian had done to me. How could he think I was making it up? I sat in silence and fumed, blocking so as to keep Xyla from catching my thoughts. I didn't want to upset her when her time was so near.

"And yet," Yallick finally muttered, "perhaps it does make sense at that."

I looked at him sharply. He still sat on the ground, leaning back against the dragon, with his eyes closed. I wondered whether he even knew he'd spoken aloud.

"Why don't you just ask Xyla?" I snapped. "She'll tell you I'm not lying."

He opened his eyes and looked at me again. I stared back, willing myself not to blink or flinch.

"If you speak the truth, then you of all people will understand my need of caution. If you are deceiving me, there is nothing to prove you have not deceived her, too."

It felt like being stabbed. My insides clenched in the face of Yallick's wrath the same as they had when I'd first found myself without my maejic. I managed to rise to my feet.

"I *will* find a way to prove to you that I'm telling the truth." And I walked away. I wanted nothing more than to storm out of the cave, but I knew that this was exactly what he expected me to do, and I decided to prove him wrong.

Instead, I went to check on Oleeda and Traz.

"It is good to see you up and about, my dear," Oleeda said, giving me a warm look that didn't do much to make me feel better. "Can you tell me what happened?"

"I don't want to talk about it right now," I grumbled.

She raised her eyebrows. "As you wish."

Honestly, I half-hoped she'd argue with me, make me repeat the story to her. I imagined her hanging on every word, gasping at all the right places, nodding sympathetically. Believing me. The way I'd expected Yallick to. Instead, I just asked, "Can I make you some tea? Some breakfast?"

"I am ahead of you there." She motioned toward the table, where Traz sat lethargically sipping a mug of steaming tea. "I do not know what is going on, Donavah, so I hesitate to say anything." She threw a glance toward Yallick, who still sat by Xyla, deep in thought. Or maybe asleep. "But you were marvelous yesterday. More so, I suspect, than I know. I honestly expected you to be dead today, you were declining so rapidly. Instead you are quite well. Strong, even. The progress you have made in the past few months since we met—it is amazing. Beyond what I ever expected, beyond what Yallick ever hoped."

At the mention of his name, something inside me snapped. I had done everything—everything!—he'd ever instructed. I could have returned to Roylinn Academy, taken the easy way, but he'd convinced me that I had more to offer the world than Roylinn could have prepared me for. So I had accepted his challenge. And for what? Certainly I had learned more in those first weeks than I would have in six months at Roylinn, and that had been exciting, even fun. But then it all fell apart when we'd gone on the run. Worst of all was the agony— physical, emotional, and spiritual—that Anazian had caused. And now Yallick refused to believe me!

As these thoughts raced through my head, Oleeda just watched me with a quizzical expression on her face. It seemed as if she wanted to say something but wasn't sure how to phrase it.

The atmosphere of the cave suddenly grew stifling. I grabbed my cloak. A long walk seemed just the thing. I hoped that Yallick might call me back, but he didn't.

When I got outside, I embraced the cold air. I breathed deeply, letting the chill cleanse the tension from me. A splotch of color on the periphery of my vision caught my attention—the melted bits of the meditation candles from the night before. I went over and stood again in the center of my circle.

Two mages, a man and a woman, walked past, startling me. They just nodded politely, but curiosity burned in their eyes. As if they wanted to know how it was that I was up and about but were afraid to ask. Which was fine, for I wouldn't have told them. They hurried into the cave.

Closing my eyes, I began the familiar routine. Clear my thoughts. Find my calm center. Open my inner senses. Absorb the power of the earth, the air, the life all around.

The power cocooned me with silken strands of energy. I reached out my hands and accepted the gift. My skin tingled. My hair stood out on end. I laughed.

When I opened my eyes, I saw that the sun had risen almost to noon. I'd stood there uninterrupted far longer than I'd realized, well over two hours. Now I felt energized, alive, in harmony with the life vibration around me.

The life vibration! Yes, there it was. Everywhere. I stepped out of the circle and walked. Away. Anywhere. I listened to the voices of the trees as the wind rustled their branches and leaves, the song of the insects burrowing their way through life. Here and there I caught the signature of small creatures, hidden away under the blanket of snow, awaiting the stir-rings of Spring.

And there, so elusive that I almost doubted it entirely, the gossamer thread that indeed presaged the coming of Spring. I laughed aloud again, and the sound of it—sound coming from my own lips and vocal chords—echoed through the woods.

Nowhere did I detect any negative vibrations, and that made me feel even more joyful. With nothing to fear, I could relax my guard.

As if my very thought cursed the sense of peace, a shiver brushed across the forest. I halted. Closed my eyes so I could better focus my inner senses. Something unfamiliar to the woods, but not necessarily dangerous.

Then everything around me froze, as if it were holding its breath in anticipation.

Right behind me, a dog barked.

I turned around just in time to be knocked to the ground by a brown and white . . .

"Chase?" I couldn't believe it! He licked my face as I hugged his wriggling body. His doggy breath was warm on my cheeks. I sat up and held him in my lap, stroking him, scratching under his chin, enjoying the feel of his short, soft coat on the palms of my hands. And I waited for Grey to appear, knowing he couldn't be far behind his dog.

Moments later, I felt his vibration. Strong, sure, and steady. I thought it a little strange that I recognized it immediately, when it had taken me awhile to begin to recognize Traz's. But it was unmistakably Grey. I rose to my feet.

When he pushed through the underbrush and saw me standing there, his face lit up in surprise and, I hoped, pleasure. Chase barked, and now that my maejic had returned, I sensed the pride he felt, as if he'd found me all on his own.

"Well, I did." And his voice in my head sounded just as I'd imagined it would: raspy, confident, and jovial. Nothing like the gentle roar that was Xyla's voice.

"Donavah!'" Grey said, standing there staring. "I don't believe it. Well, I mean, I do believe it, because we were looking for . . ." His voice trailed off.

I smiled. And spoke. "It's great to see you. And *I* really don't believe it."

His eyes widened. "You've got your voice back." He looked at my hands, which I raised to shoulder level, wiggling my fingers.

"As good as new," I said.

"I'm glad." Then his face fell a little. "I just wish . . . well, you know, that I'd been able to help."

Chase walked over and rubbed his head against Grey's thigh. Grey automatically reached down and scratched behind the dog's ears. It was such an endearing exchange— perfect communication between a man and his dog. Somehow, it brought back warm memories of the time back in Grey's house, when I'd been helpless and unable to speak, and yet we'd still found companionship with each other.

"I missed you." It came out of my mouth before I realized I was speaking aloud.

I blushed and turned my head away slightly. Well, the words had been spoken and couldn't be taken back now. I faced Grey with a small smile, only to find him blushing, too.

After a short, awkward pause, I cleared my throat. "So, how did you find us . . . me?"

Grey shrugged. "Just tracked you."

"Very funny. We flew here."

He gave me a half grin. "I have my ways." Chase barked. "And my dog."

"You don't actually expect me to believe that a dog can track a flying dragon, do you?" I chuckled to take the sting out of my words. "Besides, it must have taken you days to cover ground we flew over in hours."

"Weeks, really. Fourteen days walking once I found someone to look after Hallin. Couldn't ride him, with that injury and all."

I scowled. Weeks? I must have been ill a lot longer than I'd thought. I tried to remember the passing days, but it was all mostly a blur.

"Hey, are you all right?" Grey took a step toward me.

"Oh. Yes. I'm fine. Just a little cold. Let's walk, and we can catch up on news."

It turned out to be much more difficult to tell Grey my story than I'd expected. Without being able to tell him anything about maejic and my ability to speak with animals, much less about why we were in the company of a dragon, there wasn't much to tell. And the last thing I wanted to admit to him was that I'd had to heal myself in the end.

His story, too, was patchy and full of holes. He couldn't give me a decent explanation about how he'd managed to "track" a flying dragon. He muttered something about traces of residue that I wouldn't understand. Not at all satisfactory.

As we walked along in silence, I wondered whether we'd ever be able to communicate openly. I looked sidelong at him. He moved with such grace and restrained power. I smiled.

Then, unexpectedly, "Look, maybe I shouldn't have come."

My stomach sank. "No. No. I'm glad you did."

We stopped walking and he stood facing me. "It's . . . it's just that I thought . . ." He closed his eyes and let out a breath. "I don't know what I thought."

I took his hands in mine. "Grey." He looked back at me, and I fancied I could see reflections of the sun in his eyes. "Grey, I'm serious. I'm *really* glad you're here. Things are just . . . strange right now."

He snorted. "You can say that again."

I came to a quick decision. "I'll prove it. I'll tell you everything. I've trusted you with my life; it's only fair that I should trust you with my soul, too."

A long pause. "All right. Me, too. Fair's fair."

"Let's find somewhere warm. The whole story, and I mean the *whole* story, is long."

He nodded once and smiled. Maybe everything would be all right after all. We started walking, and this time, he held my hand.

"Donavah!" Xyla's voice inside my head was so loud it seemed to echo in the woods. "It's time."

I halted. "Xyla? The eggs?"

"Come quickly!"

Aloud, I said, "Grey, we have to go back to the cave. Now! Hurry!"

I took off, retracing the footsteps in the snow, Grey on my heels asking what in the world could have happened.

✦

The air carries the first stirrings of Spring, and still we wait. In expectation of the final battle, our power pools in the ether. I grow drunk on its essence.

I shall see you soon, my son. I await you.

Nineteen

Apparently sensing my urgency, Grey didn't ask any more questions. Chase ran ahead of us, easily following the trail. We sped past the place where Grey and I had met, and on, on, on to Xyla.

When we finally got to the cave, I was surprised to find a crowd of maybe thirty or so mages gathered outside. Traz stood to one side, his back to the group, warming his hands over a small fire. No one had noticed our arrival, so I went over to Traz.

"What's going on?" I gasped, pressing the heel of my hand into my side. "Why is everyone out here?"

"Dunno," he said, shrugging his shoulders. "Xyla made everyone leave, even Oleeda and Yallick. Even me." He frowned at the flames.

I gripped his shoulder in sympathy and gave him a little shake. "I'm sure it's just, you know, a female thing."

He scowled at me. Then he saw Grey. "Hey, who's that? Why's he here?"

I introduced them. Grey stuck out his hand, but it was a moment or two before Traz took it.

"Grey saved my life, Traz, and sometime soon I'll tell you all about it." I pushed down the resentment that rose inside me at the memory of Yallick's disbelief. "And Traz is my very best friend in the whole world, Grey." Traz brightened up at that. "*And* he saved my brother. He and Xyla. I'll tell *you* all about *that* soon."

Then Xyla spoke to me. "Donavah, come quickly."

"I have to go to her," I said. Before I left, though, I whispered in Traz's ear, "Don't say anything about maejic." And without waiting for his response, I dashed to the cave.

Yallick stood outside looking in, a half-worried, half-baffled expression on his face. I didn't say anything but ran past as if he weren't there. Just let him try to stop me, I thought.

Xyla lay in the back of cave, her sides heaving with the labor of her contractions. I'd seen plenty of animals give birth, even a snake once, and I knew what to expect, or so I thought.

She lifted her head a little and looked at me. "I wished for you to be here, little one. I am glad you arrived in time."

"Me, too. But why have you made everyone wait outside? It's cold out there, and they'd rather be here with you anyway."

"They have angered you, and that angers me."

That took a moment to sink in. I was only mad at Yallick, and I'd tried to hide that from the dragon.

"No, Xyla, I'm not angry at all of them. Why do you think . . . ?"

"I sense your anger, but not your thoughts." Just then a huge wave rippled across her belly.

"Oh, Xyla, let them come in. Don't worry about what's going on inside my head now. They're excited to see your eggs. None of us has ever seen a dragon, well, you know."

She let out a bellow that must have been a call to the mages, because the lot of them came rushing in. Within moments, I was surrounded by a large group of people, mostly strangers, all of whom had their eyes fixed on Xyla.

A movement at the front of the cave caught my eye. Grey had come partway inside, but, as if the sight of the dragon were too much for him, he'd frozen in place. Chase hung back, not coming inside at all. As I watched, Grey backed out slowly. I took a step to follow him, to ask him to come back, when a huge cry of delight rose up behind me. Should I follow Grey or tend to Xyla? I really, really wanted to see the eggs, but I was worried Grey would slip away and I'd never see him again.

Then the noise rose behind me as people began to exclaim in astonishment. A high-pitched creel echoed off the walls. I turned to see what was happening.

"It can't be!"

"I don't understand."

"Has there ever been such a thing?"

"It must be a sign."

"But of what?"

I squeezed past the people to see for myself what was going on.

Xyla had stopped straining for the moment and instead was focusing all of her attention on something at her side. But instead of the large egg I expected to see, there was a tiny dragon, the same size Xyla had been when she first hatched.

I took a step closer. "Xyla? How . . . what's going on?"

She pulled her gaze away from the baby and looked at me with a soft gleam in her eye. "The little ones are coming."

"That's not what I mean and you know it. What about . . . eggs? What happened to the eggs?"

Yallick's gravelly voice came from behind me. "Live birth." It was scarcely a whisper, almost a prayer.

"But how?" I asked, my anger forgotten for the moment.

"Legend has it that the red dragons gave live birth to their young instead of laying eggs. I suppose I should have guessed, but Xyla herself was hatched."

"Would that be the same red dragons who . . ." I trailed off.

Yallick finished for me. "Breathed fire."

I turned to look back at Xyla. Everything suddenly seemed much more enormous than it had been before. It felt as if the whole world were watching, anticipating some momentous change.

Then the feeling evaporated as another baby dragon crept out from behind Xyla. I took yet another step closer.

"Yes, you may." Xyla answered my unasked question.

I couldn't help grinning as I moved forward, slowly approaching the nearest baby. Once it noticed me, I stopped moving to let it get used to my presence. Xyla crooned reassuringly, and it looked up at her. I blew a little air through my teeth, making a soft *ssss* noise to attract the little one's attention again. It gave a quizzical cheep, and I took another step nearer. And another, and another, and then it was within reach.

I picked it—him—up, careful not to tweak his wings. His skin was still birth-damp, and I wiped his body down with my sleeve. I sat on the ground and set him on my lap. He looked up at me, blinking. With gentle fingertips, I wiped his face. He seemed to enjoy my touch and when I stopped, he pushed his head against my hand, just like a cat when you stop petting it.

I smiled, lost in wonder. All of my recent difficulties seemed to fade into insignificance in the presence of the miracle of new life.

The next thing I knew, two more baby dragons came over to investigate. Soon they were crawling all over me, while I laughed harder and harder at their antics. My laughter was echoed inside my head by Xyla, who seemed quite charmed with her own offspring.

"You egotistical beast," I said, trying to look up at her but finding my view obscured by wings, tails, and lithe, writhing bodies.

"It is the dawning of a new age," she replied. Again her laughter filled my head as I lay back and let the little ones cover me.

Then I saw Yallick standing nearby and for the first time became aware of all the mages watching. I gulped, suddenly self-conscious. Disentangling myself from dragons, I rose to my feet and brushed the dust from my clothes. The first one I'd handled gurgled up at me and plucked at my knee. One of his claws went through the heavy fabric and scratched me painfully. I picked him up, and as I held him, he made a noise deep in his chest that reminded me of a cat purring.

Hours passed, and more and more baby dragons filled the space around Xyla. Eventually, she said, "Twenty-three," in a self-satisfied tone.

I gasped in amazement. "Twenty-three babies?" I tried to count, but they were all wriggling around far too much. "Twenty-three! Xyla, that's amazing!"

"As I said, a new age."

"Well, Xyla," Yallick said aloud. "You have given us rather a surprise."

She turned her gaze on him. "I require food now."

Yallick looked taken aback, and I choked back a laugh. But before he could reply, someone spoke from the mouth of the cave.

"I have meat." Grey's voice echoed off the walls, and everyone turned to see.

He'd fashioned a sort of sledge and was pulling it behind him. Animal carcasses were piled high, and I wondered how he'd managed to hunt so successfully in just a few hours.

Xyla let out a bellow and stood up. Seeing her standing there, drawn to her full height and surrounded by her tiny young almost took my breath away.

Grey approached with the sledge, and the mages made way for him. He looked up at Xyla, his eyes a little wide. The baby dragons pounced on the meat, and I wondered whether Xyla herself would actually get any at all. Yallick, deciding that the show was over, began to herd everyone out. I slipped my arm through Grey's and walked out with him.

"How did you know . . ." I started to ask, but Yallick interrupted.

"Donavah, it is time for afternoon meditation," he said, but I noticed that he was actually looking at Grey as he spoke. "There is another cave just beyond that outcrop that we can use." He went on ahead.

I sighed. "I've got to go," I said to Grey, "but I'll be back."

"I need to meditate, too. I'll find somewhere sheltered in the woods. It's what I'm used to, after all." He gave me a shy smile.

I followed the path in the direction Yallick had pointed and found the cave easily. Traz stood just inside, holding a bundle in his arms.

"Here," he said, grinning. "I thought you might like to see an old friend."

"My pack!" I took it from him and held it to my chest. "I wondered what happened to it. Thanks for keeping it for me."

"Well, not me, exactly. Yallick. I did go through it once we got here to take out any food," and he pinched his nose, "but I didn't look at anything. I promise."

I grabbed him with one arm and pulled him into a hug. "That's all right, Traz. Nothing private anyway. I'm just glad to get it back!"

Traz had called it an old friend, and silly as it seemed, that's exactly what it felt like. I wandered into the cave. Two separate pools of candlelight glimmered where Yallick and Oleeda were beginning their meditation sessions. I went to the far side and sat on the ground.

My pack didn't actually have much in it: some cooking gear, my waterskin, a few packets of herbs. And the traveling set of meditation candles that Kibee had given me before I set out on the journey to try to rescue Breyard.

I pulled a pair of candles randomly from the leather bag. Lavender for clarity and red for love. A warm feeling rose inside me as I lit them. I might be far, far away from every familiar part of my life, but here was a unifying thread.

I slipped easily into the routine. Within only moments, it was as if I were outside myself, drawing on the power of the forest life, pulling it toward me, almost as if I were hoarding it into my soul. It swirled inside me, sparking and igniting, expanding and multiplying, until my spirit felt it would burst with joy.

A sense of peace then settled on me. I looked around the dimly lit cave. Yallick sat nearby, facing me, and his eyes reflected glints of candlelight. I blew out my own candles, rose to my feet, and walked out of the cave.

Grey stood nearby, waiting. I held out a hand, and he took it in his. Chase trotted ahead of us as we walked back to Xyla's cave to look in on the babies again. Grey squeezed my hand, and I knew everything was going to be all right.

✦

I do not like to admit it, but Donavah's story of Anazian's treachery must be true. I cannot begin to imagine why he has betrayed us. Yet no other explanation fits the events.

That he tried to kill her is the final proof, if any were needed, that she does indeed have a vital task to fulfill.

But my disbelief of her has angered Donavah, and I must work hard to regain her trust. I am a stubborn fool sometimes.

And now that interfering young man has appeared, and I fear he will steal Donavah away. They spend far too much time together. It cannot be long now before the two of them discover that Grey is maejic, too.

The End

About the Author

The first thing I remember writing was a poem celebrating my seventh birthday. I still remember the first line, but nothing can induce me to repeat it. My poetry, with few exceptions, has not improved.

I discovered that writing is something I'm good at when I was in fifth grade, and that's when I decided I wanted to be a writer when I grew up. In seventh grade, I read *The Outsiders* by S.E. Hinton, and that's when I decided I wanted to write for teenagers.

And now, I really do write for teenagers. Only thing is, I haven't grown up yet. Nor do I intend to.

Please visit my website
http://www.teriegarrison.com